Duty

BY ALAN BISHOP

Poetry
Leafmeal

Biography
Gentleman Rider: A Life of Joyce Cary

Editions
Joyce Cary: *Cock Jarvis*
Joyce Cary: *Selected Essays*
Vera Brittain: *Chronicle of Youth (War Diary 1913–1917)*
Vera Brittain: *Chronicle of Friendship (Diary of the Thirties 1932–1939)*
Vera Brittain: *Wartime Chronicle (Diary 1939–1945)*,
with Y. Aleksandra Bennett
Vera Brittain & Winifred Holtby: *Testament of a Generation
(Selected Journalism)*, with Paul Berry
Vera Brittain and Four Friends: *Letters from a Lost Generation*,
with Mark Bostridge
Henry Smalley Sarson: *Reliquary: Poetry of the First World War*

BY PETER ABBOT

Novels
Librarian
Gukurahundi: Voice of the Lord
Hamiltonians
Quintet: A Novel of COVID-19
Armistice: A Love Story
Plague Year
Duty

Short Stories
Gaiety

Duty

A Novel

Peter Abbot

Rock's Mills Press
Oakville, Ontario
2021

Published by
Rock's Mills Press
www.rocksmillspress.com

Copyright © 2021 by Peter Abbot.
All rights reserved. This book or parts thereof may not be reproduced in any form, stored in any retrieval system, or transmitted in any form by any means—electronic, mechanical, photocopying, recording, or otherwise—without prior written permission of the publisher.

This is a work of fiction. Names, characters, places, and incidents either are the products of the author's imagination or are used fictitiously. Any resemblance to actual persons, living or dead, businesses, companies, events, or locales is entirely coincidental.

For information, please contact us at customer.service@rocksmillspress.com.

For Judith, with love

And in memory of Paul Berry

Acknowledgement

This novel was inspired and influenced by the reading of many historical accounts of the two World Wars, and especially by Vera Brittain's record, in her Diaries, Letters and Journalism (edited by Alan Bishop), of her own experiences and observations.

What in our lives is burnt
In the fire of this?
The heart's dear granary?
The much we shall miss?
(Isaac Rosenberg, "August 1914")

They also serve who only stand and wait.
(John Milton, Sonnet XVII)

All that was so long ago. But …
(Clare Leighton, Preface to Vera Brittain, *Chronicle of Youth*)

Duty

PART ONE

Chapter One

'Hullo, I'm Phoebe, who are you?'
Jane, lying back on grass, opened her eyes to brightness.
'Do you live around here?' the voice continued. 'I don't think I've ever met you before. You're very pretty, wish I had long fair hair like you, and just hanging loose I mean – but Mutti won't let me.'
Jane had sat up. There was a sudden shrill cry of many voices: 'Howzat!'
'Oh, is that Arnold out? No, looks like the Ref's signaling a bye, can you see? I need new glasses, Mutti says and I think she's right for once. It's very glary too, isn't it?'
'Yes, such a lovely lovely *lovely* day. That's why I was lying on the grass, looking at the clouds passing by.'
'And counting the butterflies. Do you always say things three times? No, don't get up, I'll sit in this chair.' Phoebe was waving ostentatiously. 'Daddy's looking this way. I think he must be wondering what I'm doing, but I told him I'm feeling restless and I just wanted to wander about for a while. Cricket is a bit boring, isn't it, even if your brother is Captain. But since Mummy died, Daddy watches Arnie and me like a hawk.'
'Oh, I'm sorry.'
'What about?'
'Well – your mother.'
'Oh, that was two years ago, Daddy's re-married, Mutti's my

step-mother – and we're quite recovered now, Arnie and me. She was a rather distant mother anyway. So where are you at school? You're not wearing a uniform like I have to, lucky you' – she smoothed her blue skirt, then lay down carefully beside Jane – 'and you still haven't told me your name. Though I think I know who you are, your Father works for my Father and I've seen you cycling through the village.'

'Jane. I'm Jane.'

'Oh, plain Jane! No, that's rude – sorry, I take that back. So what are you going to be? When you grow up. *If* you grow up. See, I'm still being rude – once I start, I can't stop. Mummy used to say that.'

Jane smiled and leaned towards the other girl, pummeling her arm lightly. They were lying on a grassy rise overlooking a Cricket-pitch – not far from their Fathers; who were sitting beside each other on picnic-chairs and disagreeing gently but forcefully about the merits of the two cricket-teams, as well as, more circumspectly, their sons' sporting abilities and achievements. Mutti was in the Club-house behind the two girls, supervising the provision of tea and refreshments: half-time was imminent.

'*I'm* going to be a Writer. A Poet, I think. Or a Journalist. How about you?'

'Oh.' Jane was impressed. 'Well, I'm still deciding. Maybe a Nurse. My Father says that's a good profession for a woman. Better than a teacher or a secretary, he says. Didn't use to be, he says, but, you know – Florence Nightingale – '

'But isn't your Father Daddy's – So, how can he know? Are you a Feminist? They're just troublemakers, Daddy says, because they can't find a man, and Arnie agrees with him.'

'Oh no – I don't think so – and there's Olive Schreiner too, have you read *The Story of an African Farm*? It's my favourite novel.'

'I don't read a lot of books – no time, there's horse-riding and parties and tennis, now that term's ending and summer's starting – life's getting so busy, and the summer always goes so fast. Usually we go over to Europe in the summer now, to visit Mutti's family in Germany or Daddy's in England. Mummy used to say there's too little time to do even half the things one wants to do. "Life's like a passing shadow" she used to say "and you'll pass with it if you don't get a move on". I remember some of her opinions. And she used to write poems. But my grandmother, she was a *famous* feminist, Mummy said – and she wrote quite a lot of books – novels mainly, nobody reads them now, of course, and Daddy says they're embarrassing anyway, which used to annoy Mummy – but they're in our Library and I'm sure you can borrow them if you'd like to. '

'Thank you, Phoebe.' Jane sat up and clasped her hands round her knees. 'Look, they're coming off the pitch, must be half-time. But you said your Grandmother's books – nobody reads them now? Are they in the local library?'

'I have no idea. Oh, but you could be a Literary Executor, like my Uncle Michael was – Mummy said she would be so happy if I did something useful like that, instead of trying to be a Poet, and Daddy said so too. She left all the books and letters in good order, Daddy said. And so you could read them all if you want to. Arnold, my Brother, he isn't interested, of course – he said that. He's eighteen, two years older than me, and he wants to be a Lawyer and a big Land-owner like Daddy is, and make lots of money. Or that's what Daddy thinks. So you could read those old books if you want to, they're all in our Library. How old are you?'

'Eighteen.'

'I'm sixteen, everyone thinks I'm older.'

'What's his name? Your Brother.'

'I told you – Arnold. But I call him Skunk because his feet smell.'

Jane giggled. 'Oh. All boys are dirty and messy, Mum used to say. But they get better when they get older and get interested in girls. Which hasn't happened yet with *my* dear Brother –

we're twins, did I say that? – no, I don't think so. Look, there he is, he's waving at us which I don't think he should be doing, but he's a bit of a rebel, Mum always says that, and so he gets into trouble often. His name is Edwin, which he *hates*, he says it's one of the commonest boys' names, half his friends are called Edwin, he'd rather be called Marmaduke – '

'*Marmaduke!* Is that him over there? Come on, let's go and refresh ourselves and you can introduce me to him and your Father on the way, and I'll introduce you to *my* Father and Arnold. And here he is.' She caught hold of her Father's nearer arm. 'Daddy, this is Jane – who is *not* plain, as you can see, and we're going to be great friends – and I hope – Oh we didn't talk about that, did we, Jane? – I hope that we can be at the same school from next term.' But Phoebe's Father had turned away, buttonholed by a friend.

Another man looked down at her, smiling. 'And I'm Jane's Father. Now you know why she's not plain! And I hope she hasn't been regaling you with her usual dreamy nonsense. Come on, then, you two! I'm thirsty and I expect you are too.'

The two girls made their way to the Club-house, obediently following Jane's Father. At one end of a long table sat Lady Marston, Phoebe's Step-mother, wielding a large silver teapot. 'Hullo, Girls' she said. 'I can see you have made a new friend, Phoebe. I hope that you were both watching the Game. If you were not, Arnold's friend Edwin's side scored more than a century, I have been told – he what-do-you-call-it Opened, is that correct, and scored fifty-five runs, so do not forget to congratulate him.' Her hair was carefully coiffed, bright red lipstick surrounded her brilliant smile, and her slim body was accentuated by a silken skirt. Jane was impressed.

'Oh, Mutti, this is Jane –?'

'Erlinger,' Jane said.

Phoebe's Step-mother smiled again, while she carefully poured tea from the large teapot. 'Oh and you are Edwin's Sister! And what a pretty name – Jane – and your surname as well. Originally German. And of course our dear King is of German blood. And so was his Mother. I am sure you know all about that. Our beloved Queen Victoria! You must come to have Tea with us, soon – Phoebe will enjoy your company. Do you live locally?'

'Yes. On Trafalgar Road, opposite the Catholic Church. My Father is employed by your Husband, I think. He's an Accountant and Land-agent.'

'Oh. Oh, yes. Of course. I have met your Father. A very pleasant man, he is over there talking to Mrs Etherton, and I was so sorry to hear about your Mother's illness, I hope it is not severe, please tell her we wish that she will recover soon. Well, our house is not far for you to walk, is it? Otherwise our Chauffeur can drive you in the Rolls-Royce. If it is raining.'

'Thank you.' Balancing two cups of tea and two plates of cucumber sandwiches on a small silver tray, Jane made her careful way to a table.

'I'll just see if I can unearth Beloved Brother' Phoebe announced as she marched away.

Edwin, in slightly-soiled cricket whites, and with a glass of orange-juice, suddenly emerged from the chattering throng. He sat down on the chair beside Jane.

'So – what did you think?'

'Of your big score? Congratulations, Eddie. How many boundaries altogether?'

'Oh, only the one six, but also two fours. Not bad, I think – the pitch is putrid, bumpy as hell.'

'What's he saying? Excuses, excuses – don't believe a word he says. Wait till *we're* batting – then you'll all see some *real* cricket!' – Arnold and Phoebe had appeared. They sat down opposite Jane and Edwin. 'I hope he hasn't been filling your ears with lies – it's Jane, isn't it? ' Arnold smiled and winked at her. 'My know-it-all Little Sister has already told me how pretty and charming you are, and I see that for once she wasn't lying. Of course Edwin has said nothing. He is *so* discreet! I'm Arnold, Phoebe will have told you that I'm her Brilliant Big Brother, and I'm very glad to meet you. Of course you know how hugely significant this Match is: it's nearly the end of Term – only Speech Night and Leavers' Ball and Cadet Camp left for us to salivate over before Summer Vac! No more academic grind, and we're the last two Houses left standing, and in an hour or so only *one* House will be standing – and the winner will be -'

'Buckingham! Up with Buckingham! Down with Westminster!' and Edward leaned forward to seize Arnold's lemonade.

'Oh, come on now, don't fight, you two' Phoebe intervened. 'Arnold, will you please tell Jane who we are. Seriously.'

'Oh, you mean, not only how important our Family is – that's Mutti's job, isn't it? Now, Jane, the truth is that our Family is a major cause of dissension and disaster, not only locally and regionally, but nationally and internationally. And who knows – if the great British Empire that misrules half the world, the greatest Empire the world has ever known! and if it should weaken in the face of the righteous indignation of all its long-suffering subject-races – '

'Oh, Arnie, stop, stop! Don't listen to him, Jane – he does this sort of thing whenever he feels like it, just to cause annoyance and consternation.'

'It's all right, Phoebe.' Jane smiled at Arnold, thinking 'I rather like him. He's lively. And he's very good-looking.'

'Anyway, they're summoning us' Edwin said. 'Let battle re-commence!'

Chapter Two

'No, *no,* Mutti! *Please,* please! That hurts!'

'Well, you say you wanted plaits, and so that is what you are getting: plaits.'

Phoebe gazed at herself in the mirror. 'Only because you won't let me wear my hair long! Now I'm beginning to look like a little house-frau.'

'House-frau*lein,*' Lady Marston corrected, smiling at her step-daughter's anguished expression. 'You *said* you wanted plaits – now, did you not say that? And I agreed: you will look very lovely, wait and see, when you are all dressed up and ready. We do not have very much time, Darling. Daddy will be *very* proud of you, and so will I. And so will your Edwin. I am glad he will be sitting with us when Daddy gives his Speech – yet I am sorry that his Mother is too sick, in hospital, very sick, I have been told – and his Father must care for her of course. I do like your Edwin, *meine kleine* Darling, even if you think I do not. He is two years older than you, like Arnold. And Arnold said he is clever, and also musical. However – '

'But you're so what's the word, judgemental, Mutti. And he *is* very clever: Arnold says he has won half the Leaving Prizes, without even trying. And a Scholarship to Oxford – Balliol College, no less! And he plays the piano so well – Bach and Mozart and Beethoven and Schubert, I love listening to him, and you would too, Mutti. I'm sure he'd love to accompany you when you sing those Schubert *lieder* that you adore, so why don't we have a little concert – And he sings and acts so well - '

'Yes, and he does seem to be a nice boy, I do not disagree with you, my Darling – but remember also his Father is – '

'Oh, you're going to be snobbish again, Mutti, I wish you'd just give him a chance – Of course I know his Father sort-of works for Daddy, he's a business agent, I think – isn't that what Daddy said? So I'm surprised you don't try to stop the two of us even *talking* to each other, Edwin and me – but you should at least give him a chance, he's very talented and very clever, ask Arnie.'

'And I wish *he'd* give *us* a chance. Imagine arguing about Politics with your Father! On the first occasion when he is invited to Dinner! Was *that* good manners? Of course he would not know – unless you have told him? No? – that I was born and grew up in Germany? I am glad that at least he did not criticise the Kaiser – though he did say that the German Navy is "increasingly threatening". And what about the British Navy, isn't *it* "increasingly threatening"? What does he know about international – '

'Oh, Mutti, I don't want to quarrel with you, or anyone else. I just want to enjoy the evening, and especially watching them get their awards, Eddie and Arnie. And of course hearing Daddy's speech.' She giggled suddenly. 'Eddie and Arnie! They sound just like a Music-hall act, don't you think?'

'You think that is funny? All right – Pax! Little harridan that you are! Your Father did warn me, he said you will always have more sensibility than sense – I think he was referring to the dreadful other Jane, that writer who is *not* your friend, I hope. No? You said you admired her novel what-is-it-called, *Prejudice*? And there, what do you think? *I* think you will look *beautiful*, and everybody will be asking who you are – and Edwin should be very proud and grateful to be your what-is-it, Accompanist? All the other boys will envy. So come, give your ugly old *frau* a kiss. And now you must hurry to get ready.'

Speech Night! The whole School was primed for a presentation of noble brilliance on this annual Great Occasion – as primed as, one by one, all the other Public Schools of England had been or would be. Much attention had been lavished on every detail of the evening, since of course the School's importance and reputation would be under parental scrutiny. So – Which Gilbert and Sullivan had been performed and acclaimed this year? I must have something to talk to Eddie about, Phoebe was thinking. They did *The Mikado* three years ago, my favourite G&S, but this year I didn't feel like going – and surely, yes, it was *The Pirates of Penzance* –

And there is Eddie, up on the stage! He didn't even tell me he'd be performing, singing that solo, and looking so handsome, and singing so splendidly, the hero of the evening! 'There'll always be an England – ' How well he sung that! And then, after the Choir sang some sea-shanties, he was applauded for his violin solo – something by Sir Edward Elgar, who composed those *Enigma Variations* that Eddie played me on the record-player after explaining how each variation represented one of Elgar's friends! Phoebe sat entranced, and Jane clasped her hand.

Then there was the Interval, during which Parents and Masters proceeded to the Marston Hall to chat and drink sherry. In the Ladies' Powder-room, Jane was congratulated effusively for her Brother's performances; while Phoebe smiled and chattered with a friend. And yes –

The best was yet to come! When everyone was back in their seats, the Headmaster stood at the podium clearing his throat until the audience was completely silent; and then he announced that this year the Speech would be delivered by Sir Arthur Marston – who needs no introduction and is so greatly admired by all of us for his generosity and leadership. And he is an Old Boy! Fervent applause, while Sir Arthur rose and made his way to the podium. Once there, he cleared his throat, then spoke forcefully.

In this time of uncertain international peace, we should take pride in the leadership of our great Empire, the largest and most admired, the finest ever known to History! And yet there may be some concern that Great Britain's example of Peace and Progress around the world is under attack, flouted more and more openly, and by a Nation or Nations that he would not name. International Peace is under threat as never before, we must all be watchful, we must all be ready at any time to play our part in the defence of our great Nation. That is our duty, our *duty*. 'Dulce et decorum est pro patria mori.'

Jane, sitting beside Phoebe, was aware that Lady Marston was leaning forward and listening intently to her husband.

The Speech ended, and was loudly applauded. Then the Headmaster resumed his position at the podium, as Sir Arthur moved to a table laden with Books. The Prize-winners were announced and the Books presented to the Boys who had won them. Edwin received three Books, Arnold four – 'almost a clean sweep by the two of them!' Phoebe whispered to Jane.

And then the National Anthem, with the School Choir bellowing their request that God should save our King, and send him Victorious, Happy and Glorious to – where? Jane unexpectedly wondered – oh yes, of course, to Reign Over Us! And she smiled at Lady Marston, who was looking hard at her.

Chapter Three

'Edwin, do you love me? *Really* love me? Now that War is – '

'Yes. Oh, yes!' He caressed her arm, holding her tight against him. 'Possible? Likely? Imminent? Yes, War certainly seems to be all that. And *I* declare that I love you, I love you, I love you. Phoebe, I do love you.'

'Well, kiss me, then. Properly this time, on my mouth.'

In fine sunny weather, they had walked to the coast, a mile or so from the frowning grey-stone Marston residence, and climbed a low cliff rising above the beach. There, on a grassy knoll, they had sat and talked, and talked, and talked, for almost two hours; and he had at last kissed her, tentatively; and now, in the warm glow of sunset, they had lapsed into a series of calm silences, between quiet questions and hesitant answers.

'And you do really want to go?' She turned to look into his eyes. '*Really*?'

'Yes, Darling. No. Yes. As I said, it's my *duty*. If there's a War. Yes, I suppose I'm not as committed to military things as Arnold is. But, as your Father said in his Speech, and he said it again the other night at Dinner, you remember – he said that we must *all* be always ready and willing to defend our Great Nation. It's our duty, our *duty!*'

And Phoebe again, later: 'But you didn't say – you didn't say, Eddie, your duty to What, or Who? To England, to the King, to your School, to your Honour, to your Family – ? You must have an Object.'

'Oh, all of the above, darling. And I won't be alone, will I? All my friends, including of course your own dear Brother, I'm sure they all feel the same way. Even more strongly than *I* do. *Much* more strongly than I do. Some of them think I'm just an effete Musician, and I do love singing, and playing the piano, even accompanying your Mama Mutti, as you know. But I'm also an Englishman, and so I love Cricket, and Rugger, and our great Empire that's making the whole world a better place, and – So let's make the best of the time we have. After Cadet Camp next week, I'll have to sign up and go into training, I expect – if your dear Pater's right and there's a War on by then – or is definitely coming. And, as I said, I hope Arnold and I could be in the same Regiment, and I suppose we'd be sent to fight on the Continent. Belgium, France. Flanders! That's where the Germans will probably strike first. And we'd be sent there, to support the regular Army, after more training. All we O.T.C. types. Otherwise, why did we do all that marching and learning to use rifles and bayonets? Actually, I'm looking forward to it, in a way – even if it means I can't go to University for a year or two.

'But why am I thinking this way? Must be your revered Pater's influence. Duty and all that. But probably none of it will happen after all and we shouldn't even be talking like this. Or *I* shouldn't. You say I'm a Pacifist. It's just that – well, War can be so *destructive*. We both know that – but *you* are the *true* Pacifist! Because, well, partly because you are a woman, and women don't fight. And you'd be too young, anyway. And think of the Thirty Years' War! But this one would be short, we know that. Our Army and Navy are the best in the world. My Father told me about the Boer War, and about some poems he read recently in *Punch*, they were Sonnets, I think, about fighting for England and Democracy. Why don't you write some poems? You're good at English.'

Phoebe smiled. Then turned again towards Edwin.

'What a long speech! I didn't tell you before, but Daddy says he won't allow Arnold to sign up if there's a War, and they both got angry and had a big fight, Daddy and Arnold. I think Mutti may sympathise with Arnold, in a way – she was born in Germany, I think I told you that? She's not our real mother, as you know – she was born and lived in Germany until she was I think about my age; I tell her she's Militaristic, and she once said she has some distant Aristocratic relatives who are Officers in the German Army. She wanted Edwin and me to meet them but now it's too late anyway. I'm puzzled that she doesn't mind Arnold fighting against the Germans, if there really *is* a war. That's what she says, I think. Maybe she just doesn't want to offend Daddy. I thought Daddy *would* mind, because of what people might think and say. But maybe I'm wrong. And anyway, maybe nothing will happen. I hope so. And as you say, *I'm* the Pacifist, aren't I? I can't bear the thought of people being killed – whether they are English or German. Or French, or Italian! So – '

Silence. Except for a few shouts, and the hiss of waves, in the distance.

'Well, your speech was as long as mine, I think. Now it's getting late, we'd better walk home before they send the Police to find us.' Edwin pulled away from Phoebe, and stood up. 'But what does Arnold say about all of that? I know he has some Pacifist tendencies. *He* told me that, it isn't a secret.'

'Oh, you know more about the way he thinks than I do, probably. Pacifist tendencies? I think he just cares about suffering more than many people do. He's a Vegetarian, you know? And he reads a lot, Tolstoy's one of his favourite writers – you know, *War and Peace*. But I don't think – '

'Yes, I did know. Caused a bit of a stir at School – his Pacifist tendencies. In one of our Debates, he spoke in favour of Bertrand Russell and his gang. In fact, after that he was challenged to a fight in the House, but the Senior Master got wind of it and intervened. So – I don't completely agree with Arnold on pacifism or whatever, but I do respect him. He's like you, my dear Phoebe: sticks to his principles. And of course you *are* siblings. I wonder how it will work out for him? I hope well; as I say, I do respect his values – even if I don't always agree with them.'

'And mine? What about *my* principles?'

'Oh, as I said, Girls don't have to fight for their country.'

'So they don't count? Be careful, Mr Erlinger, how you answer! I'm not – '

'No, you're not, my dearest Darling – you're not, you're not, you're *not*. Now let's trudge. We're going to be very late and your Pater will be reaching for his shotgun. So we must *walk, walk!*'

They reached Marston House just after Lady Marston had sent a Servant to inform the local Police that her daughter and a friend were Missing.

'Oh, *Mutti*!' Phoebe lamented. 'We're only a *little* late.'

'*Two hours late*' was the response. 'Now your Father will conduct you to the Police-station to explain, and after that he will deliver *you* to your home, Edwin. I thought the better of both of you!' And she turned away from them ostentatiously.

'Sorry, old boy! My fault!' Phoebe whispered, nudging Edwin.

'Oh, don't worry' he responded when they were out of earshot. 'Your Mother doesn't like me anyway. Jane's much more her cup of tea. Though of course we are both worthless members of a lower class, aren't we?'

'Oh, that's silly, I'll slap you next time you say anything like that! Whatever my dearly beloved Step-mother says, she can think what she likes, and I will think what *I* like. Come here.' She kissed him lightly. 'And here comes Daddy, so you'd better buck up now, and bow submissively, and touch your forelock.'

Chapter Four

'But *why*, Daddy? You know he wants to go. All his friends are going, and Eddie thinks he and Arnold will be going together, his Father can arrange that. Eddie says it would dishonour our family if he doesn't go, and I think so too!'

'Enough for now, Jane. Please. So much tension – your Mother's in Hospital, as you well know, and here in the Village everyone's running round in circles yelling at everyone else – and War has only *just* been declared! Surely we can discuss the situation calmly, later on. I haven't even had a chance to talk to Sir Arthur yet.'

'Won't you see him this evening at your Board meeting? But sorry, Daddy, I don't want to upset you or Mummy – and Edwin's gone for a long walk, so I can't talk to *him*. Maybe he's with Phoebe. He seems to be infatuated with her. I think I'll go across to the Park and read more *Middlemarch* – George Eliot always seems to calm me down; and maybe there'll be someone I know there.'

'All right. Just don't forget to come back in time for Supper – I don't want your Mother to get even more worried and upset. Remember, she's had a bad time in one war already, and lost her Father and Brothers in it, and seen some terrible things in South Africa – so we mustn't – Anyway, *I'll* be here if she needs me – they promised they'd send for me if she does. And I'll know where you are.'

'Thank you, Daddy.' Jane put on a jersey and set out for the Park.

There she found a gathering of local citizens who were talking loudly together about the implications of War. As the Anglo-Boer War had been the only major conflict in which Great Britain had participated for more than a decade, there was a widespread sense of confused anticipation – even excitement. Jane avoided joining in the gathering. After smiling and waving to some neighbours, she found a comfortable bench, and sat in dappled late-afternoon sunlight reading about Dorothea's tribulations as Casaubon's deluded admirer.

Until Arnold's voice broke into her consciousness. 'So this is where the bookish Miss Erlinger may be found on a glorious summer afternoon! May I sit beside you?' And he sat beside her.

'Oh. Arnold. Of course.' She closed her book and smiled wanly at him.

'Why so sad, pretty Damsel? On such a splendidly historic afternoon, welcomed by so many! Have you not heard the News – ?'

'Oh. Yes I have, of course. Isn't it – well, exciting?'

'"Exciting"? Not the word I would have expected from you. I thought you were a Pacifist, Edwin always assured me you were. A *true* Pacifist. So why "exciting"?'

'No, *you're* the Pacifist! Aren't you? I think violence and killing and suffering are horrible, *but* – '

'*But* necessary? *But* acceptable? *But* good for British manhood? *But* better than the alternative, whatever that may be? *But* ordained by God?'

'Oh, Arnold, don't! It's not a joking matter. My Father is worried about Mummy, she's in hospital, I think you know that – And about Edwin – he says he won't allow Edwin to join up. And that would destroy our reputation in this Village, wouldn't it? – and in your Father's Company? – so – '

'Whoa, whoa, Jane! And you may know that my situation will almost certainly be even worse. My parents are in total conflict, fighting the war before it even gets going, and I don't know how it will all end. Remember, my Stepmother is German – or rather, she grew up in Germany – and my Father, despite his big Speech the other night, full of all that patriotic stuff – I know he worries, he even told me this, some time ago – He worries that I'll get myself killed and then who will there be to continue the blessed Family name? – and run the Company, and make more and more money from it, and be admired as the great Proprietor and Benefactor and local Bigwig? – etcetera, etcetera – Oh, slap me, kick me, Jane! But don't think I wouldn't have all-out war with Sir Arthur Marston before I ever got to fire a gun at the Kaiser.'

'Well. So that's how it is. Oh, Arnold – Now what?'

He laughed. 'Now I catch my breath and check my heartbeat. And you – well, I don't know what girls do when they feel emotion. Smile and flap their eyelashes?'

'And that's *extremely* rude, Sir Arnold Marston the Ineffable!'

'Where do you get such big words? "Ineffable"! And you didn't even go to School, did you? A proper school. Or that's what your ineffable Brother told me. He said – '

Jane stood up suddenly. 'I would like to walk, Sir Arnold. Would you care to accompany me? In Jane Austen, that always leads to confidences and over-hearings and misunderstandings, of course. But I have things to tell you. And simultaneously I feel a need to exercise, and indeed I have for too long been sitting here in thrall to the ineffable George Eliot. How she would have loved to present your rude communications, with suitable authorial implications and better grammar, to her admiring readers!'

He stood up and offered her his arm.

'First' she said, as they set off, 'my Mother. You may have observed that she is quiet and retiring, a dutiful Wife and Mother. And often ill. As she is now. But not to be underestimated! I will tell you just a few things about her. Growing up in Cape Town, she lost her Father and both her Brothers in conflict during the Boer War. A destitute young woman when my Father met her – he was on some Mission or other, maybe on behalf of your Father's Company. But she had been fortunate to meet Olive Schreiner – you know who she was? Yes, she wrote *The Story of an African Farm,* one of the greatest novels, all too rarely read now – and another book, *Woman and Labour,* which was also deeply loved by my Mother – and by me. That's why I'm a Suffragist – Women must have the Vote! Olive Schreiner befriended my Mother and, seeing that she was a young girl in a difficult situation, helped her financially, and employed her as a literary assistant, in South Africa and then in England – and gave her a mass of her letters and manuscripts. Which are in a trunk somewhere in our house, waiting to be sorted and organized. So – Yes, my Father met and married my Mother in Cape Town. And Edward and I were born there. Though of course I don't remember much of that time, I was too young, believe it or not.'

'Quite a story! And is that why you had a South African Tutor – what was his name, Pieter Pienaar? – Edwin told me about him. How he would come from London whenever he could, sometimes, in summer, for weeks and weeks.'

'Oh. Then he probably also told you how, in our early years, he would tease poor Piet. 'Please can I Pee Naar? Piet, please can I Pee Naar?' I thought that was horrible, embarrassing. But Piet put up with it, mainly because he liked and admired my Mother, I think – they even spoke Afrikaans together; and also he enjoyed talking to her about Olive Schreiner, and of course South Africa generally. And then there was Piet's friend Willem Potgieter, who would sometimes come with him from London – did Eddie tell you about poor Potgieter? Eddie would whine and say 'Can I Pee Naar in your Pot, Gieter?' So very embarrassing. And he's still such a Jackass, isn't he, sometimes? But I love him, I couldn't lose him. It would be such a dreadful loss, how could I go on living? I hate the thought of him going to fight the Kaiser. But who's going to care about *my* opinion?'

They walked in silence for a while. Then Arnold said 'Well – what chance do we have when our Lords and Masters decide to start an International Conflict – using us as pawns? Only way out of it would be claiming officially to be a Pacifist, I suppose – and then, if that was even allowed, you'd be despised as a coward by everyone, your friends, your family, everybody – Anyway, *you'll* be out of it, Jane.'

'Will I? If you and Edwin go off to war, then I will too.'

'You? How could *you*? Oh – as a Nurse, you mean, like Florence Nightingale? Would your parents allow that?'

Jane felt close to tears. 'Arnold – let's not say any more about it now. Thank you for our talk. And cheering me up. I think. But I'd better be going home. Daddy, and maybe Mummy, would expect Eddie and me to go to Evensong, and I'd pray for Mummy to get better, and also I'd pray Please God, Stop the War! Stop the War! – And it'll be twilight soon. Oh – listen – '

Some in the crowd had started singing the National Anthem. Vociferously.

PART TWO

Chapter Five

April 14th, 1915.

Dear Jane,

Here we are in Flanders near the town that the Men call W–, known correctly as Y–. Almost all the local place-names that I have heard here are challenging to an English tongue and so they often get mangled into a sort of doggerel version – except for Passchendaele, that name is only too clear and memorable, I think! Anyway, you don't want to read about Flemish place-names, and I expect you're doing what you said you would do, following the War news every day in the newspaper.

Then you will know that another big battle seems to be starting near here, the Huns attacking the Allied Army and trying to break through into France. But we are determined to stop them, and protect Y– , which they are attacking with their big guns. There's a rumour that we may be moved closer to Y– soon. Meanwhile we wait, and I have been able to see our surroundings, where the Enemy were in control before. The countryside is a dreadful muddy mess, and I saw some corpses which made me think about what you were saying when we talked about the War, remember? Not long after Speech Day, when War had just been declared and crowds had gathered in the Park? I remember that so well and I hope you do too, we talked for a short time and I think I knew then how much I love you.

So I hope you are keeping well, my dearest Jane. I have also written a short letter to the Pater, and Mutti and Phoebe. Also to HM at the School – he asked us to give him our news whenever we could. So my Conscience is Clear! For the moment, anyway. And now I must gather some men to check the Wire, this is just routine at the moment, because the Enemy are not nearby, but it's important for us to keep the Men busy.

*Sincerely,
Arnold Marston*

Jane finished reading the letter aloud to Phoebe, and then sighed deeply. They were in the Park, on a fine Spring day, sitting side by side on a bench.

After a few moments, Phoebe turned to her. 'Thank you for reading that to me, Jane. I know he probably won't find time to write letters to me as well as Daddy and Mutti, so I'm really grateful. When Edwin has recovered and can go over, and join the fighting – in the same Regiment, he is hoping, as you know – I'll be able to read from *his* letters – read them to *you*, I mean. Oh, dear Jane – I feel I've grown up a bit, not into being as mature and kind as you are, but better than the silly egotistical Phoebe of last year, who was always just chattering about this or that? I hope Eddie would agree! But here I am forgetting – '

'What?'

'About *you*, and your situation. I was so sorry about your Mother, Jane, so truly sorry. How are you coping, you and your Father? And does Eddie know?'

'Daddy and I were so grateful that you and your Father came to the Funeral, Phoebe. And then your Father found the nurse, and she has been such a boon – and Connie, she's our cook and house-keeper, she's been *essential* – Daddy was too devastated to manage, even though I tried my best to help. But the Baby, you must come and meet him soon, he just gurgles and wriggles and seems to smile at everything – '

'Does Edwin know?'

Jane was silent for a few moments. Phoebe wondered if she had been thoughtless, had pushed her friend too hard – 'Sorry, Jane, I shouldn't have asked that. You see how thoughtless I can still be.'

'Oh, no, Phoebe. I should control myself better. It was such a shock, you see. Of course I knew that Mummy wasn't well, she spent so much time in bed, and then in hospital, but even before that she was so – absent. But I had no idea – you know, that Mummy was pregnant – and Daddy never said. So I feel guilty as well as sad. I could have helped Mummy more, I *should* have helped her so much more. I remember that once, when the two of us went for a walk on the golf-course, months ago, she suddenly stopped and looked into my eyes and said "There are things we don't talk about, darling – " And she hesitated, and then smiled and took my hand, and we walked on. And now – Well, of course, it's too late now. But I told Daddy I would always look after my little Brother – can you guess what his name is?'

'I *know* what it is. Mutti told me, of course she would've found out, she always does. *Thomas*. Is that right? Thomas the twin – a little brother for Edwin. And of course for you. Edwin would – well, after losing his Mother, and now – being in hospital – '

'He doesn't know yet – Daddy thinks it would be a dangerous distraction, that's what he said. And now Arnold – a big battle is being expected, apparently – as the newspapers are saying – and we must wait until – But oh, Phoebe, I don't know what is the right thing to do – everything's so complicated – What do you think?'

Jane was weeping. Phoebe took her hand and kissed it.

April 23rd, 1915.

My dear Jane,
I hope you have received my last few letters. Thank you for yours, I am not sure they have all reached me, as we have moved quite often. Mine have been very short, sorry, but there is always so much to do, as well as getting to know the Men.

Our big news is that we will be going into the Trenches again tomorrow – but don't worry, I'm not worried, because it has been quiet for a while – I think the Germans may have realized that we will not be running away so they can just march into France and capture Paris! However, there have been a few casualties, one was a school-friend called Robert who was killed when he was on patrol two evenings ago. You may have met him at that last Speech Night, he accompanied me when I sang that G&S song.

What about you? I hope you are keeping well, and are having fine spring weather! I received quite a long letter from Pheebs last week and replied yesterday (but not at anything like the same length!). Your last letter came at the same time, and THIS is my hurried response – in fact, I must rush off as I have just been summoned by Garrod, one of the other Officers.

Well, it wasn't anything very important, so here I am back to complete my little Missive!

I have just remembered that I haven't told you about meeting not just ONE poet but TWO poets, when I went last week to near Wipers with the Colonel (who seems to have taken a fancy to me! Must be my Exceptional Charm and Impressive Bearing, what what!). They were both Canadians! But they didn't know each other before I introduced them. So you see, I can appreciate Poetry too, must be an inherited ability! – from Mummy not Pater, but don't tell him – or Mutti, you know how she always defers to him! Anyway, one of the Canadian poets, the younger one, he's only a few years older than me and is actually English – he said he was in Canada when War was declared, and he signed up immediately in the Canadian Army. I liked him a lot! He showed me one of the poems he is writing about the Refugees who we saw fleeing out of Ypres in a big crowd – and like me, like anyone with a heart, he pitied them because they were now in great danger, as well as being homeless, their houses destroyed by the German bombs that have been raining down. One of his poems was about a child just eleven years old who was killed by a bomb just as her family were leaving their home to join all the other refugees. The older Canadian, who is a Gunnery Officer, an older man called I think Major Macrae, was very cut up by the death of a friend, and I remember that the poem he was writing, which we persuaded him to recite, was about how we must avenge everybody who has been killed by the German Army – the poem started, if I remember it aright, 'In Flanders fields poppies grow, between our crosses row on row' and of course we do see poppies growing everywhere, especially in what they call No Man's Land, and their bright red flowers do make one think of blood. Then the Colonel and I had to hurry back to our Lines. Sorry to meander, I am writing some poetry, trying to, and I wonder if you are still doing that?

I must stop. There is always something important to be done here! But it is always so good to think of you and the happy times we had, and will have, together!

Your Friend,
Arnold Marston

'He sounds busy but happy, do you agree?' Phoebe commented. 'Also it must be quite a relief to get away from those trenches for a while. What did you think?'

'Yes. I hope he's being careful – going into Ypres must be very risky, when the Germans are bombing it and the people are fleeing. And the newspaper says a big German attack has now begun, and they have even been using poison-gas, although that's against international law.'

'But Arnold and the other Officers must be used to recognizing and avoiding danger by now, and he was with a Superior Officer. *I'm* wondering when Edwin will be fit again and the Army will decide about *his* future. He must be getting impatient: he said something like that in his last letter, when he was still in hospital in Scotland. Has he said that to you too, Jane? He's still hoping to be with Arnold, in the same regiment, isn't he?'

'Yes, he did say that, Phoebe. But I'm afraid I haven't written much to him recently, it just seemed too difficult and too painful at first, after Mummy's death, and I didn't want to upset him while he was in hospital. He joked that he was under enemy attack – you know, German Measles.'

'Yes. He made the same joke when Daddy was in Glasgow and was allowed to visit him. Actually, Daddy said he thought Edwin was still very poorly, looking quite peaky.'

'But, Phoebe, he did write to me, and of course to our Dad, about Mummy's death, and that was very kind and thoughtful of him. When he was so sick.' Jane smiled wanly.

'Well, I should be going home, Jane – Mutti always makes such a fuss if she thinks I'm late. And it looks as if it might rain, so maybe we should both set off for home. Please give Arnold my love when you reply, and tell him not to forget his admiring Little Sister – though of course I know how busy he is. And good wishes to Baby Thomas!' Who was now asleep, in the perambulator beside his Big Sister.

Jane remained in the Park for a while longer. After rereading Arnold's letter, she carefully refolded it and replaced it in its envelope. Then, pushing the pram with its silent occupant, she walked home slowly, her mind troubled by circling thoughts of her Mother's death, of her Little Brother, of Edwin's uncertain and Arnold's dangerous situation.

Next day, late in the morning, the telephone rang just when Jane, holding Thomas and cooing encouraging words as the

Nurse watched smilingly, had succeeded in persuading him, snorting and puffing, to suck milk from a bottle.

Then the baby was taken gently but firmly from her. Puzzled, Jane held the proffered telephone to her ear. Silence. And then she knew.

'Oh, Jane' – Phoebe was struggling to talk. 'Oh, Jane – the telegram arrived just a little while ago and Daddy's just devastated – Arnold – oh, Arnold, he's been killed in the trenches during a big attack near Ypres, the telegram says – he was gassed, it was gas, poison-gas – '

'Phoebe – I'm sorry, I'm so very sorry – Oh, Arnold!' and Jane stood up, weeping. 'I'll come as soon as I can – Please, Phoebe, can I – can I do anything to help? Please – '

'I'll meet you in the Park in half-an-hour. Daddy's so – desperate – Mutti called the Doctor and he sent him to bed with some pills I think, and a hot drink – but he was wailing, I've never heard a man wailing, it was awful – just wailing and wailing – '

When Phoebe arrived, the two young women clung to each other, weeping.

Chapter Six

Jane, on her knees, was playing a game of Catch with Thomas, who was staggering around the room in spurts of gurgling laughter. 'Oh, you naughty boy! Come here at once and let me dress you and make you respectable, what a *bad* boy you are!' She stood up, so as to sit back on the sofa. Chortling, Tom threw himself into her outstretched arms, just as the phone rang.

'Hullo, it's Phoebe. Is that *your* heavy breathing, Jane?'

'Oh, I'm just having a game with Tom. But it's lovely to hear your voice. Where are you?'

'At home. Well, it's hardly that for me now. But Daddy has been telephoning to say he needs to see me and that I must have forgotten the way home! – though, now I'm here, even Mutti seems to want to just ignore me, and the house feels like a morgue, so cold and dreary. Let's meet? If you can tear yourself away from your progeny for half-an-hour.'

'Of course, Phoebe. See you in the Park in an hour or so – eleven-thirty? I hope you'll be wearing your Uniform? And I'll have to bring Progeny with me as this is Martha's day off.'

'Wait and see! Tell Tom I expect his best behaviour. He must be a really big boy by now? And don't forget to bring Edwin's latest communication, he's not writing to *me* – where is he, anyway? No, don't answer now! Eleven-thirty in the Park.'

As she sat on the familiar bench near the Park entrance, Jane unfolded Edwin's latest letter, wondering whether she should read all of it to Phoebe. Especially the reference to their apparent estrangement – Edwin's from Phoebe. 'I hope all is well with Phoebe' he had written. 'She's probably as busy & preoccupied as I am, so many demands & responsibilities. But she could at least try to send a few words. So if you see her – '

And suddenly she did see Phoebe. 'Oh, you *are* wearing your uniform! It's lovely!'

Phoebe sat down heavily beside her. 'No, it's *not* "loverly", it's not even practical, it's just a damn inconvenience, you're always having to worry about whether it's getting dirty – the way I am now, just sitting here! And the cap or whatever it is slips about, and your damn hair flops in front of your eyes just when Sister comes round the corner. Oh, you look shocked' – she took Jane's hand and kissed it – 'but we're all learning, us Nurses, how to swear like Navvies – or like Tommies – not *your* Tommy, I can see he's still a little cherub, but some of our grateful Patients swear a lot, even at us, *especially* at us, when they're in pain, poor creatures – Oh, Jane, I can't tell you how good it is to be with you. And now I'll stop talking so you can *start* talking. How is your Father?'

'Not so good, Phoebe. He's been depressed, more and more depressed, I think, ever since Mummy's death and the news of Arnold's death. And so many other deaths. Like me, he has troubling dreams that Arnold's still alive somewhere, and also nightmares about how he died, the struggle to breathe after being gassed. Oh, sorry – I shouldn't – It's really all about Edwin actually. Worrying about him. *Your* Father has been so kind and – so amazingly courageous, even tries to cheer Daddy up, takes him to the pub and they play darts and so on, but – well, I worry about him. And he won't have anything to do with Tom – his own son, but of course Tom's not Edwin, and I suppose he's more like a grandson of his than a son, but that's – well, it's hurtful, and I worry about Tom, when he's old enough to notice.'

'Oh, Jane, dear Jane. At least that won't be for a while. And have you been hearing from Edwin at all? All we know is that he said his Regiment was likely to be sent into the Trenches near the Somme River, and now the newspapers are saying that there will soon be a big battle in that area, huge enemy forces are gathering. Oh, this War, this War!'

'Yes, Edwin said as much in his last letter, a short one – he said there was always so much to do, and especially when another big battle is brewing, that's what he said. I'll read it to you, it came the other day and I was just re-reading it when you telephoned.'

'Oh, no need to read it now. If you can spare it for me to read to Daddy and Mutti, I'll return it before I go back to London tomorrow. I know how much they'll appreciate that, they have been worrying so much, like me.' And she held out her hand for the letter Jane had been reading.

'I'll just find the envelope. It must be in my bag. I have been keeping all the letters, from Edwin and Arnold, so that maybe they can even be published after the War is over – Daddy said that they are so well-written, which is no surprise, and they will preserve memories of the War for future generations. But this one is just about waiting, and duties and preparations, and uncertainty – '

'Oh, Jane. Please. I can see that it's very private, and of course I know how you and Edwin – like Arnold and me – ' and she hugged Jane tightly for a few moments. 'Just read me what you can, when you feel you can, and if you can copy out some parts of his earlier letters and send them to Daddy, I'll be so grateful. And now I'd better go home for lunch before Mutti tells the Police that I'm missing – or some other diligently observant citizen reports that "There's a marauding Nurse in the Park", maybe a murderess in nurse's uniform! You must remember when something like that happened to Edwin and me, we were just a bit late, and we had to explain and apologise to the Police, because Mutti blew the whistle on us! Dear old Mutti!'

A few nights later, after Jane had put Thomas to bed and sung him to sleep, the phone rang, loudly piercing the silence. Jane picked it up hastily.

'Jane!' It was Phoebe. 'He's here! Right here!'

'Who?'

'*Edwin!* Who else? Edwin, Edwin! Here, in this Hospital, I've just been talking to him, he's sleeping now but he asked me to let you know he has survived, and say he hopes to see you soon! Can you come up to Town tomorrow morning?'

'Oh, yes I must! I *must!* Oh – God has answered our prayers.'

'Well, don't get soppy now. Of course I don't accept that God has anything to do with it. But we can argue later. And I'll telephone home now and suggest to Daddy that he brings you, he's coming up to London tomorrow and he knows where the Hospital is, and I told him which ward Eddie's in. Maybe your Father too – '

'Oh, thank you, Phoebe. How am I going to sleep tonight? And I'll have to make arrangements for Tom. Connie, that's who helps me with the cooking and house-cleaning, her father is sick again, but she said she'd always look after Tom in any emergency – So – Anyway, good night, Phoebe, and thank you, thank you.'

Edwin's face, Jane immediately noticed, was very thin and pale. His left hand fluttered against the sheet as he tried to talk. His right arm was bandaged against his emaciated chest, and one of his legs was encased in plaster and suspended from the ceiling.

'Thank you for coming, you can see I'm not too destroyed, just a bullet through my right elbow, and of course my bloody left leg is useless but they say it'll come back and I hope they're right! I was lucky, so many casualties, don't they say it was the worst casualty list so far, but the Enemy's losses must be much worse by far. According to the newspapers.' He stopped, to cough and clear his throat.

'Oh, Edwin,' Phoebe said, 'just rest, don't talk and exhaust yourself. We won't stay long, and we'll come back often, and I'm always very close – so don't try to tell us everything now, just rest. Jane and I are just so very glad to be with you and know you are safe, and we'll come back often.'

He smiled and tried to lean forward. 'Lovely to see you two. And Jane, you look – and good old Pheebs, and Sir Arthur – thank you all for coming to see me! And Dad sent a message.'

As he fell back against the pillows, Jane put her right hand against his left arm, trying not to cry. 'Oh, Edwin, we're all so very glad, so relieved – '

'So you think I should believe in God now?' and he smiled again. But Jane sensed his bitterness. 'Of course,' he continued, 'God could have saved all those others too, and some might even think that He could have stopped the whole bloody slaughter from happening.'

A nurse came to take his temperature, and then looked meaningfully at them.

Arnold's Father cleared his throat. 'Well, I think we should go now, Edwin. Mutti sends her love and you know we'll all be thinking of you. We are so proud of you, Edwin. Your School and your Country are so proud of you. Our undefeated Warrior! So goodbye for now, we'll be back tomorrow' and he looked meaningfully at Phoebe, who leaned down to kiss Edwin's forehead.

'Don't hurry' Phoebe whispered to Jane as she followed her Father into the corridor.

Silence. Until Edwin said harshly 'Well – what, Jane? Here we are. Or *are* we? Is that really you? I've thought so much about you, and Arnold, and all the happy times we had together – but what is there to say now? I don't know if I'll be good for anything at all when I recover, *if* I recover.'

Jane wept. 'Edwin, don't! Please. I love you. I'll always love you.'

She leaned down and kissed him – not on his cheek or on his forehead, but on his lips.

Chapter Seven

'So was I an orphan, Mum?'

'Of course not, Tom. What a question! But then maybe, especially as you'll soon be off to Oxford – well, let's have a real conversation for once tonight, after Tea, you and Dad and me. And Julia, if she wants to join in. All right? I've got things I want to show you, too.'

'Yes, of course, if you like – But I hope it won't be too long? I said I'd meet Julian and the others in the pub later.'

'And I hope you won't be drinking more than a couple of pints – you promised, remember!'

'Oh, you always bring that up, Mum. That was only once! And it was inexperience, that's all. Of course I don't want to end up a wastrel and a drunkard, to use one of Dad's favourite warnings. Oh, and I've just remembered – Neville wanted to get together, he says he needs my invaluable advice.'

'*Your* "invaluable advice"!' Tom's Father exclaimed. 'Has he any idea how asinine, that's one of your favourite words, isn't it? – how *asinine* you can be, Tom! Better to send your friend to the Reverend Mister Manson-Smith for what he's paid to do, Manson-Smith I mean. Of course *I* don't get paid for anything, even your Mother expects my priceless advice to be free.'

'Oh, now, you two, stop it! No more skirmishing – is that one of your favourite Scandinavian words, Tom? Just telephone him and invite him to join us for Dinner tomorrow night. All right?'

'Yes. But it's *not* Scandinavian, my dear Mother, it's, surprise surprise, from Old French. And Scaramouche, have you heard of him, what an ignoramus you are, how did I ever get accepted by Balliol when my maternal mental inheritance is so – ? Obviously I couldn't owe it to my *paternal* inheritance, and the fact that Dad is, wait for it, a mere History Teacher, and the fact that – '

'A source of wonder indeed, my dear son' his Father intervened. 'Unless you have discovered that I paid the College a large sum, out of your inheritance of course. Julia, why don't you say anything? Women are not expected to be silent in this household, as your Mother, our Ardent Feminist and disciple of the redoubtable Mrs Pankhurst, will assure you.'

Julia sighed. 'Oh, Dad. Oh, Mum. Oh, Tommy. Speak and be silent, I say. Poor Cordelia! And I'm off to do my homework. Miss Bentley is a dragon, or should that be dragoness, Daddy? She definitely breathes fire and brimstone. Derivation, Thomas? Brimstone? See – he's reduced to silence, thank you, Beowulf.' And she went.

Early next evening, Jane placed a cardboard box on the kitchen table. She opened it as Tom joined her.

'I hope this won't take long, Mum. Neville's always on time.'

'No, everything's ready, your Mother has been slaving at the stove all afternoon. Oh, enough of Tomfoolery, that's entirely your preserve – and your Father's. Neither of you have any respect for me. But I just have something I want to show you. However, first I have something to *tell* you, my dear Thomas. Are you ready? Now – Listen carefully: I am not your Mother, you are not my Son.'

'What do you mean, Mum? Are you joking?'

'No, darling. I'm not. Now, we'll just take this calmly. Listen. Sooner or later, you would have found out, and really, I think, I should have told you earlier. Your Father thought that, and maybe he was right. But it's not bad news, and it doesn't change anything fundamental. That's what I think, and I hope you will too. So listen: I am your Sister, your Big Sister, and you are also my beloved Son. All right?'

Thomas was staring at her. 'You're joking. Aren't you? You must be. It just doesn't make sense. All right, then: whose son am I – honestly?'

'Your Grandfather's. Sorry, darling, I can see what a shock this might be for you! But he was a good man. Kind and generous. I loved him very much. And you may remember him playing with you – '

'Well, not – In fact, I have only one very-early memory: Christmas, when I was – how old? Less than a year old, wasn't I? And yes, Grandfather was there, I think. Wasn't he? Or am I making this up?'

'What a good memory you have, darling. You take after him. Your Grandfather. Your Father.'

'But then, who was my *real* Mother, if you're not my Mother? I don't remember anyone else – except Aunt Phoebe, but she lived mostly in America, she just came and stayed once and never stopped talking – is she still alive?'

Jane smiled. 'Oh, very much so. She can't travel much any more, she says, but I'm hoping we can visit her, you and I, if things calm down a bit, especially in Germany, those Nazis are so troubling – have I pronounced the name correctly? Nazis? And their leader, isn't he the German Chancellor now?'

'Hitler. You mean Herr Hitler. Der Fuehrer!'

'Well, but we're getting off the point. You're too young for the next war, if there is one – I hope. But the last one, the Great War we called it, as you know – and there *was* great destruction and suffering – which we have all tried to forget as much as possible. But, Tom – there was so much suffering, so many deaths, and one of those who died was – '

'Oh, now I'm beginning to – You *adopted* me, you and Dad, didn't you? That's why you say you're not really my Mother – '

'No, darling. It's more complicated. You're my Little Brother. And Grandfather, who you hardly remember because he died when you were so small, he was, he really was, your Father. As well as *my* Father. And *your* Mother was *my* Mother. There – I've said it, after all these years.'

Tom sat silent. Then he stood up as Jane began to weep. 'Oh, Mum – I – '

'Yes, but Tom – No, please sit down again. Look, I've got two letters to read you. I must do this now, darling. I *must*. Or *you* can do it, please. Please. Here – ' She held out two envelopes to him.

Dearest Jane

It is nearly the end of November 1916, a whole year after I first joined the Regiment & was sent over here, & I am back in the trenches! After that glorious time with you – & Sir Arthur & Phoebe & Mutti & little Tom – but it was those walks and talks with you that were, & are, so precious in my memory. I seem to almost re-live them, & all our long conversations. Oh I remember so much what we said to each other, and especially I remember that long walk along the Coast, in glorious autumn weather, with waves beating against the cliffs – and I telling you that I loved you – & you saying, so quiet, that you loved me too – and then we sat for ages on that bench & talked & talked – but what did we talk about, I think mainly about our friends and families, especially Tom, & Phoebe, & our ambitions for the future when the War is over, and oh, so much else! How very much we both missed Arnold. Such precious memories, my darling – remember how I called you that, for the first time? The first of many times!

But I mustn't go on. I will be going out with some of the men to check & repair the wire in front of our trench. This place is even worse than the Somme was, all mud & mess, & corpses, I can't tell you what it's called except to remind you that I mentioned it, a village beginning with P.

I'll write again as soon as I can. Meanwhile, all my dearest love, my darling.

Edwin

Tom replaced the letter in its envelope and returned it to Jane.

'Thank you, Tom. I don't think I could have read it all through without crying. His letters still hurt me – upset me – after so long!'

'Well, I can see how moving they are, Mum. Oh – *Mum* – but you know, I don't think I can possibly think of you as my Big Sister – and I don't want to. You were always my Mother and – ' he took her hand and kissed it – 'you have given me so much, so much love, and so much more – so please let's leave things as they were. Anyway, I don't think we should let anyone, Herr Hitler or, who was it, oh yes the Kaiser, control our lives and especially our thoughts and emotions. So. Next one? Hand it over.'

Jane smiled. 'Thank you, Tom. I think I hoped you would feel that, and say that. And you know, you are about the same age as we were then, Edwin and I. But not, thank goodness, involved in a Great War, a catastrophe of catastrophes. But before you read this letter, the last he wrote me – '

'Just a moment, Mum. I wanted to ask you about all those shoe-boxes of letters. Surely they aren't just the ones you and Edwin wrote?'

'Yes, you're right, my dear Son. My dear *perceptive* son. Well – after Edwin died – and Arnold was his great friend, he had died earlier in the War – Arnold's Father and his sister Phoebe, who you have met of course, as you remembered – he asked me, when I told them I was keeping all the letters they had written me, and that I thought they were so fine, and such a superb record of the War as they had experienced it – he asked if I would like Arnold's letters to *them* as well, for safe-keeping, and of course I said Yes – and then friends of Arnold sent me letters he'd written to *them*, and letters from them to him – after Arnold's Father, Sir Arthur Marston as you know, gave a speech about Arnold and Edwin and other Boys who had been school-friends of theirs and who had served in the War. And Sir Arthur, and the Headmaster, gave me all the letters *they* had. So that's how it happened – but I never got round to – Well, there are so many letters and I didn't have a lot of time, having to chase *you* around, and then there was Julia, and – now maybe it's too late, with another War threatening – But if – Well, you won't have time at university, but maybe in the future, who knows – maybe you will read them all, which will take some time of course, and decide whether – Well, come on, now. Read this final letter, your friend will be arriving soon. The last letter Edwin wrote me. Though of course – well, he couldn't have guessed that, but he did write "Farewell", so maybe – '

November 4th 1917

My dearest Jane,

Oh, the mud, mud, mud! It gets in everywhere, your boots, your whole uniform, your eyes, your brain! But you don't want to hear my disquisition on Mud, so why am I wasting time on it? I hope the Enemy is equally tormented. By it, & by the loathsome lice. And that's enough about that. *At least we have not had to endure what they call a Battle for a while – sometimes I think of how battles used to be, knights on horseback, and man to man, not this filthy grind where you get shot through your head if you dare to try to look over the parapet. Which, let me assure you at once, is not an action I ever perform.*

Sorry to be maundering on! This life we are forced to lead – But I will stop and clear my mind, because I had intended to write you a letter worth reading! A letter about my friends and comrades who have given me so much kindness and love. I'm not talking only about now, *though you know how much my love for you, and yours for me, has shaped and blessed my life. I am thinking also about how I have been so blessed by my Mother & Father, & my friends, the best friends I could ever have had, all through my life. I love you so deeply, dearest Jane. But also Arnold – how I miss him, how much I enjoyed his company, he was the best and noblest Friend a man could ever have. Others too – the Colonel, & my batman & fellow Officers, among whom, now dead, now slaughtered during this hideous War, are four school-friends of Edwin & I. What can I say? What could I ever say. We were going to change the world, help to make it a better place. I loved them all. I love you all. I love you.*

And so, farewell.

PART THREE

Chapter Eight

'Hullo. Is that you, Jane?'
'Oh – Phoebe? Phoebe! Lovely to hear your voice!'
'After so long! Sorry about the silence. I guess it sounds silly and unconvincing to say I've been busy, but I *have*, and I haven't been in England for ages, I'm *desperately* cosmopolitan now – '
'Oh, I know you must be busy, Phoebe. I've seen your book and even read it. About your memories of nursing in the Great War. It was very interesting.'
'I hope I didn't offend you, Jane – I guess I should have asked for your permission to quote from those letters, but – the publisher said there wasn't time.'
'You knew you didn't have to do that, Phoebe. And you did thank me in the Introduction. And of course we were, *are*, friends. When will I see you? Can you come here for a few days? We could easily put you up in Tom's old room – he's – well, you wouldn't know him, of course he was just a baby, wasn't he, when you saw him last and now he's nearly twenty-one, and in Balliol College in Oxford – he's reading Philosophy, though he's more interested in English Literature, which of course he can't study – his College President said that's only what you read for relaxation, *if* you have time. What would George Eliot have said to *that*? And isn't it strange, almost as if Edwin was – you remember what strong opinions he had? And Tom looks

quite a bit like Edwin too – But, Phoebe, there's so *much* to talk about, so much to tell you – '

'Well, Jane – I'm here for only a few days, doing some interviews, and then I'll be in France and Italy – for a long article in *Happy Holidays Magazine,* do you know it? – an article all about British and American War Cemeteries – Why don't you come to London and I'll take you to lunch and we'll have a good long *chinwag,* is that the right word, about old times? I guess I'm more American now than I really appreciate.'

'Oh. Well, all right. I can take the train tomorrow morning. But I'm just a rural elderly lady now, not used to busy London streets. And I'd like you to meet my daughter, she's at school of course, in her final year, but I think I can – '

'So I'll see you tomorrow, at noon? The Empire Hotel is near Victoria Station, just across the road, in fact. I'll meet you in the Lounge there at – let's say 11:30. It'll be *lovely* to see you, Jane.'

'But who is she? And why can't she come and see *you*, surely she wants to see the village and the house she grew up in? – it's that old mansion isn't it, the one you once told Tom and me that you used to have friends who lived in it, before the War?'

'Yes. She's a very old friend, Julia, and I'm sorry she didn't have time to come here, she lives in America now, and she's quite a well-known writer and journalist. I telephoned you earlier and left a message, just to see if you could come to London with me and meet her – she's very interesting and has published a novel and might have some helpful information and advice for you, as you're so interested and so talented in writing.'

'Oh, *Mum!* I hope you didn't – Anyway, I must go. I wouldn't have been able to meet you in London tomorrow – hockey game! See you at the weekend!'

Jane sat still for a few moments, then set out for the Station.

On the way, she took herself to task. 'Phoebe will think me such an old *frau,* and of course that's what I am – but then, she's only a few years younger than me, even if she's so much more successful and competent and sophisticated. If Walter hadn't left me – but then he *did*, and after so long together, and said I was disorganised but wouldn't explain what he meant, I think I still resent that. *Disorganised!* But thank goodness, I have Tom and Julia and some real true friends – '

She was only ten minutes late, but Phoebe, smartly-dressed in a grey suit, and meticulously coiffed and made-up, looked at her watch as she smiled and stood up. 'Hi, Jane. *Wonderful* to see you, thank you so much for coming, I have such a short time between appointments so let's go across for lunch immediately and we can talk there.' She kissed Jane perfunctorily, took her hand, and led her across the street to a small Italian restaurant. 'They told me the food's good here, so it better be if they want a tip!' and she smiled brilliantly as they sat down opposite each other.

'*Now!*' and Phoebe smiled again. 'I *love* London and I'm sure you do too. I have such vivid memories from my nursing years here during the War, it was a real hard decision to emigrate to the U.S. and leave that life behind, for the major publishing company that I work for now, but it's panned out very well because they've made me a Partner, the first Woman Partner, and also I love the travelling, not many parts of the Globe I haven't visited! But I shouldn't talk about myself so much. What about *you*, Jane?' She laughed suddenly. 'Remember how I once called you Plain Jane! In those days I was often *unbearable*, wasn't I? You can be honest about that now – now that I'll soon be thirty-five and *you're* over forty! But – of course there have been hard times, what with the War and the Depression, though much worse here than in the 'States, I guess! Anyway, what about *you*? And help yourself to wine. Are you married? Yes, of course, I remember you had a little boy, he must be grown-up now. I must confess, before you ask, that I am *off* marriage: three husbands are three too many is what I always say now, but I did come out ahead, financially, in the end. Are you shocked? No, I can see that you found happiness with just *one*, what was his name, I have such a terrible memory for names?'

'Walter.'

'Oh yes, that's it. Walter. A good solid name. My father was called Arthur, *Sir* Arthur, as you may remember, and my Brother – ' She paused, turning her head away. 'I was forgetting, Jane – that you and Arnold were special friends, weren't you. And when he was killed – And then Edwin, he was *my* special friend at that time – And what a rotten time that was, wasn't it? Usually I try not to remember it. All those horribly-wounded young men, the hospital was full of them. Twenty years ago now? Incredible! Shall we drink to their memory? Here, let me pour you some wine – So. To Arnold and Edwin.'

Jane, having seen Phoebe drink two glasses of wine, lifted her glass, sipped, and tried to smile.

'Well – *drink*, Jane! Good. And now I'm afraid we should hurry, my next appointment is in half an hour.'

'Are you happy in America – and, in your work?' Jane asked hesitantly as they attacked their lamb-and-vegetables.

'Yes, I think so. Of course I could easily move into another position if I wanted – in another company – but they treat me well enough. And it's one of the best companies, always wins top awards, and of course makes lots of money. Everyone here seems to be worrying about Hitler and the Nazis and another War – I don't think that'll happen, it's all just empty chatter. But if it *does* happen, I'll be in New York. Are you nearly finished?'

'Sorry, Phoebe, I'm a slow eater.'

'Well, don't worry, I can just go ahead if necessary. But I've just remembered what I wanted to ask you, my dear Jane. This is important. All those letters during the War, like the two by Arnold that you once copied out for me – '

'The ones you used in your book?'

'Yes, the ones I *quoted*. That you gave me. You had so many, I remember you telling me – stored in shoe-boxes – I remember that detail, I think, because it amused me. *Shoe-boxes!* Anyway – The letters about the War. By our Brothers. And letters by who-was-it to your Mother – Olive somebody, South African writer you said. And Mutti told me that she'd given you all the letters *she* had kept, especially the ones by what-was-he called, the Red Baron, the pilot who shot down so many of our airmen. And then she told me, and I'm breaking my word, she made me promise not to tell anyone – *all* the letters from Arnold, when he was at School, as well as during the War up to the time he was killed – Pater gave all those to you a few years ago, didn't he? and others. Apparently he told Mutti that he knew he could trust you to keep all Arnold's letters safe. He thought they should be published, and probably Edwin's too. Other War Letters had been published, he said, and he thought that Arnold's and Edwin's were just as good if not better – I don't know why *he* didn't get them published, but he said you would keep them safe and see that they are published "at the right time", he said. And in fact, he also said you would be a good Literary Executor – I didn't even know what that was when Mutti told me he said that, a year or two before he died, but now I know, colleagues have told me what a Literary Executor does, how important he or she can be. And you know, I think Pater didn't really approve of what Arnie and Eddie wrote about the War in their letters, what a hopeless destructive mess they said it was, so he decided *you* should have the responsibility – I guess he respected you and thought he knew you well – those conversations he had with you in the Library, he once mentioned how he enjoyed them – ' She frowned suddenly, and broke off to down the last of her three glasses of wine.

Jane hesitated. 'Oh – yes, I've always kept all those Letters very carefully. I've transcribed quite a few and intend to transcribe them *all*, typing them up so people can read them easily – Edwin's writing is nearly illegible, I always told him that! And my children, Tom and Julia, they are interested in the Letters too, or Tom is – you haven't met Julia, she's about the same age *you* were when we two met – do you remember that? At the House Championship cricket-match in 1914 – just before the War started – '

'Yes. And I'm afraid I must leave you now, Jane, my next meeting is almost due. The Rolls will be waiting for me.' And Phoebe stood up. 'But could you send copies of all those letters to me? Look, here's my card with my New York address and my telephone number.'

'Oh. Well, goodbye, Phoebe – nice to see you, thank you for the lunch.'

Phoebe smiled, patted her hair, and departed.

Jane sat thinking for a few minutes. Then she carefully tore up the card Phoebe had given her. In the Ladies' Room she smiled at the mirror and said 'It's been so *lovely* to see you!'

Chapter Nine

The City was burning. Bombs exploded, throwing down buildings. Rubble and dust and flames and smoke. Sirens screamed. People ran for shelter, fell through doorways, clung to lampposts, while the world heaved around them.

Among the people was a young man, twenty-five years old, in a blue uniform. A year earlier, he had started training as a Pilot; a year later, he expected to be flying a Spitfire into some of the battles that would ultimately achieve victory by the Royal Air Force over the Luftwaffe; but at this moment, he was trying to reach his girlfriend's flat, unsure whether she would be there or with her family in their Somerset home.

Breathless, he ran round a corner – and stopped abruptly, in shock. The whole building ahead of him was in flames – the whole street, it seemed. 'Oh, God, no, no' – Was she inside, desperately trying to force a door open? – or in the cellar, which, he knew, was being used as a bomb-shelter?

He threw himself towards the building's main entrance, but was suddenly stopped, held, pulled backwards – 'Bloody stupid, want to kill yourself?'

'Please, please – my fiancée – she's – '

'– not there, she's not there, we got 'em all out, the bloody Nazi bomb didn't explode, not yet anyway, go over there to the ARP, looks like you should be up above fighting them Nazis, in that uniform, what you doing here? '

And it turned out that Emma, with other occupants of her block of flats, was sitting on a garden-chair in front of the house opposite, wrapped in a blanket and drinking tea. And chatting edgily with the neighbours who had provided the tea.

Tom ran towards her: 'Oh, thank God – oh Emma – '

Two hours later, in the late afternoon, they were on a train lurching south-west out of London. At one point, they saw a Messerschmidt shot down – not so far away; in a fury of flame, it fell into a field and exploded.

Tom held Emma to him. 'Don't look, darling.' And the train hammered onward.

'I can't help thinking about the pilot' she murmured after a while. 'And his family and friends. Oh, Tom – '

From the station they walked the short distance to her parents' home, and were welcomed with ecstatic relief.

'Darling, we've been so worried.' Emma's Mother kissed and hugged her, as her Father hobbled carefully downstairs to shake Tom's hand.

After tidying and cleaning themselves, Emma and Tom presented themselves for Tea.

'You must be hungry' her Mother said, presiding over a large plate of cucumber sandwiches. 'I hope you don't take sugar, Thomas. None of *us* do, and of course it's rationed now anyway.' She handed them cups of tea, then passed round the sandwiches.

Emma's father cleared his throat. 'What an adventure, a very *dangerous* adventure' he said. 'You must let your Mother know that you are safe, Thomas – you can use our telephone of course. If it's working.'

'Oh, thank you, Sir, but it's better if I just don't tell her. She worries so much about everything. Especially now, of course, with the Blitz. She'll think I'm at the aerodrome, I'll telephone her tomorrow. I'm just relieved that we came through all right – Emma's the brave one, that bomb destroyed the whole building more or less – '

'Well, let's not dwell on it, then – just be grateful that God was keeping you both safe, dear' and Emma's Mother hugged her yet again. 'But you must stay here with us now, at least until we can see what's happening – London's just too dangerous in this Blitz, as they're calling it. Lots of people are leaving London if they can, I hear, and of course the children have all been evacuated – we have some here in the Village, cheeky little beggars! There's one who actually burgled Lady Brantham's house and stole some money. And Thomas, you will be welcome to stay, of course, for just as long as you wish – or as long as you *can* – there's a guest room, you probably remember it from last time you were here – and Dad can lend you some clothes – that last time was actually the first time, wasn't it, soon after you met Julia at university and before you signed up for the Air Force?'

Tom was just about to reply when Emma's Father cleared his throat loudly and embarked on what Emma called 'one of his professorial disquisitions' – he was a retired Modern History Don.

'It is my opinion, although I am not a *Military* Historian, now so indispensable, but merely a common-or-garden Historian – as I say, it is my opinion that this War may last at least as long as the previous one did. The one which, you recall, was to last only a few months before Christmas 1914 and be only minimally damaging, in fact a mere opportunity for the young to stretch their muscles, but which became a Great War and over-stayed its welcome by four years and managed to kill or wound more than a few of our compatriots, as well as our antagonists, of course. I would surmise – '

'Now, dear – More tea, anyone? Sandwiches? Emma?'

'No thank you, Mummy. I think that perhaps Tom and I will take a short walk. To relax a bit before bedtime, and I want to show him the Church, we didn't have time for that when he was here before.'

'But, Thomas' – Emma's Father was not to be silenced so easily. 'I would like to show you some books of edited Letters – you will recall that you mentioned, on the first occasion you visited us, the Letters that your Mother has preserved, by combatants in the Great War, and even of the infamous Red Baron, I would really like to see those –'

'Yes, I remember, Sir. Letters written by and to my Uncle Edwin and his Friend Arnold – I think you said you knew his

Father, Sir Arthur Marston.'

'Yes, indeed. A fine old Tory. He was a member of my College at Cambridge, and I believe you said his Son was supposed to enter the College as a Scholar, but alas – such is the nature of war – '

'Maurice,' his wife broke in. 'Could we leave this until tomorrow morning, when both these young people will be rested? They must be exhausted.'

'Oh, very well. I look forward to a long conversation with you tomorrow morning, Thomas. Who knows, by then Hitler's Luftwaffe may have been defeated by the gallant English airmen you are joining, to protect our cities and defend our skies. So I shall say Good-night and sleep well, Emma, Thomas – and Celia, old girl, I suppose it is time for us to perform the nightly ritual of washing-up before we too proceed to our rest.'

Tom woke from a deep but troubled sleep. Childhood memories of the first War tangled with apprehensions about the Second, and he felt guilty about his failure to telephone his Mother and Sister, who, on second thoughts, might well have been worried about him – they would probably have heard the London bomb explosions, and might even have seen German and British aircraft in lethal combat above the Village. He wished that it had been possible for Emma and him to sleep in the same bed – or at least in the same room; that would have been scandalous a short while ago, but now – well, morality was shifting – even outside London, wasn't it? He felt lonely, cold, randy, deprived.

In the morning, Maurice was waiting for him, with a neat pile of books deployed on a table. 'As soon as you have finished Breakfast, old boy – ' and he raised his eyebrows.

Tom smiled stiffly, hoping without conviction that the arrival of Emma would distract her Father.

In fact, Tom admitted to himself later, the Old Boy was well-informed and interesting. The first topic was an account of the Red Baron's brilliant skill as a pilot, and his final downing, apparently by a Canadian pilot called, euphoniously, Billy Bishop. This led to a disquisition on the fine, even *essential*, contribution of the Empire to winning the Great War; and its significant contribution to *this* War.

Then Maurice turned to the Letters of the two young Officers, Edwin and Arnold. He would *very* greatly enjoy reading those Letters: judging by Tom's account, they were not only informative but literary in the best sense of the word. Did Tom think that his Mother might allow him to peruse them?

'Well,' Tom demurred, thinking that he might have been too unguardedly enthusiastic in his earlier comments on the Letters. Well, he would speak to his Mother as soon as possible; as he had explained earlier, she was in control of them.

Yes, she is of course the Literary Executor. She would need to be consulted. Maurice repeated that he greatly admired her commitment, and hoped that it wouldn't be very long before he could meet her and have a good long chin-wag. Oh, this intrusive obstructive destructive War! Tom thought.

And there, for the moment, that conversation ended. Emma appeared, and sat down beside Tom. 'I hope you slept well?' she enquired, constrainedly. 'At least it was a quiet night – assuming that I didn't just sleep too deeply to hear anything – bombs exploding in the distance, for instance?'

'Poor London, poor Londoners' her Mother commented. 'Why don't you two go for a walk as soon as you've finished breakfast? It looks like a *lovely* morning!'

Chapter Ten

There was a loud knocking at Jane's front door.

'Oh, darling! Is it really you? Can it be you? Oh, come here and let your Mother – ' and she held Tom tight, kissing him several times. 'But you're looking so thin – I'll have to feed you up – oh, I'm just gabbling, aren't I? Come, sit down, sit down, you must be exhausted – Put down your suitcase, take off that greatcoat – And tell me it really *is* all over, the War's *over*, at last! The Royal Family on Buckingham Palace balcony, cheering London crowds, and Mr Churchill – I heard it all on the BBC –'

'Yes, it really *is* over, Mum. Except – in the Far East, Japan – but I don't think it will be long now.'

'And then a whole new world! That's what they want, those cheering crowds – what we all want – and everything will be different, no more fighting and killing, no more lies! Do you really think that will happen, that it's even possible? Well, I hope so. That's what you fought for.'

Tom sat. 'Oh, this old sofa, I'm glad you still have it – after all those years of saying it had to go, that it was lumpy and we needed a new one.'

'I'll put the kettle on. You just relax, Tom. All the time you've been fighting Hitler, keeping England safe, as safe as possible, stopping the Blitz of London, all the bombs and destruction – the Battle of Britain – And here you are! Safe. I prayed for that. All the young men killed in the Great War – my own Brother, your Uncle Edwin – and Arnold – oh, I always thought that you are so like Edwin – and so many others were killed – but here you are –' Her voice faded as she went towards the kitchen, filled the kettle and set it on the Aga.

'But – I must telephone Julia, she'll come straight round – and Emma, have I got her name right, your girlfriend? – how is she, have you seen her yet?' as Jane reappeared, with a tray balancing teapot, cups and biscuits. She sat down heavily beside Tom and poured out two cups of tea.

'Oh, Mum. So much to tell you. Emma's parents were killed, last year – I didn't know for a while, a bomb fell right on their house, you know how the Nazi planes would just chuck out bombs if they had to turn back under attack. And Emma – I tried to contact her, but she didn't answer letters, or the telephone. So – '

'Oh, darling, I'm so sorry. I think I met her only the once, but I *really* liked her, Tom. You must make a real effort to contact her, I'll help you if I can. But before I forget – I'm getting so forgetful these days – Church! I want you to come to Communion tomorrow morning with me. The first time for how-many years, at least twenty-five! And there's a new Vicar, they say he preaches a good sermon. When God took Edwin and Arnold, my beloved Brother and his closest Friend, who was also *my* closest Friend, in that first ghastly "war-to-end-all-wars", I said to Him "God, I will never forgive you! Never!" But now He has made up for it, just a little, hasn't he – by keeping my beloved Tom safe and returning him to me!' She took his nearer hand and lifted it to her lips.

'Oh, Mum – '

'No, don't say anything. We'll have a real chin-wag later. So much to tell each other! And you're one of England's Heroes, as Mr Churchill said. The Bravest of the Brave! Now, drink up! And I must telephone Julia – I suppose I'll have to leave a message for her – so while I'm doing that, why don't you take up your things to your room? You'll find it just as you left it, four or is it five years ago, I haven't changed anything. And the Letters are still there, in the cupboard – I've got things to tell you about that later, when you've had a rest. Oh – Tom, Tom, Tom – so *wonderful* that you're *home* again!'

He slept. Then Jane was shaking him gently.

'Sorry to wake you, Tom. I know you must be tired, but if you over-sleep now you won't sleep tonight! And Julia's here –

and she wants to see and talk to her Big Brother. Oh, here she is – '

'Hullo, Tom! So wonderful that you're back – and looking so fit. When I last saw you – well, we were both in a state, my School had been bombed, remember? You tried very hard to console me, several of my Children had been killed or wounded – I still try not to think about it, it was *horrible* – I shouldn't be talking about it now, but seeing you – So, no more about that, it's a time for rejoicing, isn't it? At last it's all over!'

'And it's a lovely afternoon, so let's go and sit in the garden, my dear children.'

'Oh, and what happened about – Mum?'

'I know who you mean – Walter. He just went away, sometime after that big confrontation with *you*, Tom – he's never come back, I don't even know where he is. In Australia, I think. Probably good riddance, that's what *you* said, Julia, and maybe that's right – though he wasn't a really *bad* man. He was *your* Father, and in fact, he could be very kind, often – when he wasn't drunk, or tiddly. Oh, isn't it a lovely evening?'

Tom had been sitting very still. 'Mum, Julia – I have a confession to make, the sooner the better, probably. It's about being England's Flying-ace Hero – I'm *not*. I'm *not*. You both think I was a Spitfire Pilot. Well, I wasn't. I did want to be one, but they discovered my sight wasn't as good as I'd always thought it was. So – well, I trained instead to be a crew member in Bomber Command, and was told not to discuss that with *anyone*. I suppose I could have told you both, and sworn you to secrecy – but I didn't.'

A short silence, broken by Julia's laugh. 'Just as well – your Mother would have communicated it to the whole Village.'

'Oh, Julia, of *course* I wouldn't have. But in some ways – Remember, I *am* a pacifist, and – Well, I hope you didn't participate in the bombing of Dresden and Berlin and those other German cities, killing so many helpless German civilians, mothers and children, and destroying lovely historic buildings.

Spitfires were different, they were defending England, one could accept that, of course – But – '

'*But?* Mum, I won't argue about it, and actually I shouldn't even mention or in any way *discuss* Bomber Command – and "Bomber" Harris, you've heard of him? My boss, you could say. Until they pushed him out. Everyone now seems to think that he was *evil* and Churchill is saintly, but some of us who dropped bombs on Germany disagree. And that's all I'm going to say, it's all I *should* say. Too much already! Oh, except that the War is *not over* yet, whatever we in Europe think. The Americans are still fighting the Japanese – who attacked them at Pearl Harbor, you might remember? And *now* I'll stop. Sorry if I seem a bit – out of control, I don't usually rant, or didn't – I know it'll take me a while to get back to normal, and I'm sorry that I went on a bit.'

Jane sighed. 'I think I just want *peace*, please. For a while, anyway. And to enjoy you being safely home with us. But, Tom – meanwhile I have something to tell *you*, as well as Julia. It may seem small, hardly worth discussing, but it's been troubling me. Firstly, maybe you don't remember, or didn't know – My old friend Phoebe, Arnold's sister, suddenly appeared out of the blue just before the War began – she lives in America now, and was doing some sort of journalistic assignment in Europe, if I remember rightly. But she also suddenly demanded that I send her copies of all the Great War letters I've been looking after, for possible publication – letters by Arnold and Edwin mainly – all those written to me and Edwin, and by the two of us to Arnold and his family. Old Sir Arthur Marston summoned me and urged me – somehow he had decided I was the one to do it, I think Arnold must have told him I was a keen writer and reader, which by the way I *was!* – Anyway, he urged me to keep all the Letters safe and to edit them and try to get them published – which I did, but there didn't seem to be any interested publishers, or perhaps I didn't go about it in the right way – I was still very shy in those days, believe it or not.

The upshot was that the Letters have remained in the cupboard in your room all this time, Tom – stored in shoe-boxes, I remember Phoebe thought that was hilarious! Oh, and there are some letters by the infamous so-called Red Baron, who was the German flying ace finally shot down by I think a Canadian airman. He was a distant relative of Mutti, Arnold's stepmother. Sorry this is such a long story, but it connects with an incident a few weeks ago when a middle-aged man, who said he was an American, knocked at the front door, and asked if he could see "the famous letters". I was taken aback and, actually, a bit scared of him, and I lied that he had the wrong address. So – Well, thank you for your patient attention, my tale is done, but – and funnily enough, it was a suggestion of Emma's, your girlfriend's, Father, Tom – apparently I need a Literary Executor! He offered to find me one, in London – but then, silence, no answer to my letter replying to his, and now, alas, I know why. Well. What do you think about all this, you two? If anything.'

'I think, Mum, that you need to get professional help. I think those Letters *are* important, maybe more important than we can realise, and now is the time, with the War over at last, to do something about it. I can help you, and Tom can, depending on what his circumstances will be,' Julia looked searchingly at him 'and you shouldn't have to deal with this all on your own, Mum. That's what I think.'

Jane smiled. 'Oh, I'm not *that* old, darling. In fact, some would say I'm only middle-aged. But I take your point, it's time I got help.'

Tom agreed emphatically. 'Yes, as Emma's Father told you, a Literary Executor is what you need! Someone who gets paid for executing Writers and their Writings – Ha, ha. I remember you telling me how Writers' families could actually stop people reading and enjoying what their relatives had written, after they were dead – like Rudyard Kipling, for instance, when someone wrote a biography of him and was prevented from publishing it. Totally appalling! Though I remember, Mum, that you thought it might actually have been a good thing if we couldn't read Kipling's poems about how great and glorious the British Empire is! '

'You remember that? But it's not a joke, Tom. I wasn't advocating censorship, I was arguing *against* it, I always have. You used to be so interested in Literature – in fact, correct me if I'm mis-remembering, but didn't you say you admired Edwin's poems about the War, the ones I showed you when you were studying poetry by Rupert Brooke and Siegfried Sassoon and Wilfred Owen – you also thought that some of Arnold's poems were just as good, or even better – and I must admit that I did wonder if Sir Arthur read them after Arnold was killed, and they upset him, and that's when he decided to give me all of Arnold's writings, and my letters to Arnold, and even his diaries. Arnold would include poems with his letters, or write them *in* his letters – he could do that because he was the one who was responsible for reading and censoring letters by the Officers and Men in his Regiment – he said he'd like me to comment on his poems. And I did. Now I'm saying too much. But you can understand how precious everything he wrote was to me, and *is* to me – and also all of Edwin's letters – and why I've kept them, and valued them, all these years – And I still read them, I do, and I still weep when I read them. So now you know.'

PART FOUR

Chapter Eleven

'But, Mum, we've been worrying about you – '
'Well, *don't*! I'm fine. Everyone's so kind and helpful. I suppose they think I'm a helpless old English lady. In fact, I'm often embarrassed by it all. And I only gave you the Hospital's telephone number, Julia, for emergencies.'
'But your friend – Phoebe? How is she doing?'
'Not great, as they would say over here. The cancer seems to be quite far advanced. Mostly she just seems to want to sleep, so I sit and hold her hand and think about old times.'
'Well, please let us know how things are. We send our love – Tom and Emma and the children, and your friends Susan and Margaret, and of course me.'

When Jane went back to Phoebe, and noticed that her eyelids were flickering, she leaned close. Phoebe stirred and whispered 'Eddie, please – '
Jane took her hand, and kissed it. 'Phoebe' she said softly. 'I'm here. Jane. Remember, you asked me to come if you ever needed me, so here I am. If you need me. Your husband – Can you hear me?'
A nurse had approached silently. 'That's *lovely*, Mrs – Arlington? She's responding to you. And her husband, Jerry I think he is, he called and said he would be here soon. Why don't you take a break, get something to eat and drink in the Eatery?'

* * * * *

When Jane returned, a very overweight bald elderly man was sitting in the one chair beside Phoebe's bed. He got up with clumsy alacrity and proffered a clammy hand. 'Hi' he said. 'I'm Jerry. Her husband.'

'Oh, I'm so glad to meet you.' What a silly thing to do, she admonished herself: shaking trans-Atlantic hands across a hospital bed containing a very sick patient. 'And I'm Jane – an old friend. From England.'

'Yes. As you know, Pheebs told me about you. Who's this Eddie she keeps trying to talk to?'

'Oh. My Brother, who died in the First World War. They – knew each other well.'

And there the conversation lapsed, while they gazed at Phoebe's pale closed face.

Then Jane made another effort: 'I'm so glad you're here, Jerry. I think I should go and settle things in the hotel – it's just over the road. Or at least, I think it is. The airline bus travelled so fast, and I was feeling a bit – you know, woozy. Is that just an English word? I think I'll need a bit of a rest and – you know, unpack. I'll come back as soon as I can' and she took herself off, after ascertaining that Phoebe's eyes were still closed.

The next day, Jane was surprised to find Phoebe sitting up in her hospital bed, being fed what looked like a watery porridge.

The Nurse looked up at her. 'Oh, good morning, Mrs Hardcastle. Phoebe will be so happy to see you – yes, look at her smile!' Not much of a smile, Jane thought, and Phoebe looked puzzled rather than welcoming; but she bent down to kiss Phoebe on her forehead.

'Hullo, Phoebe. Lovely to see you, and sitting up too – Can I help with the feeding, Sister? I wasn't a nurse like Phoebe in the First World War, but I've fed a good few children in my day.'

'Well, thank you, Mrs Hardcastle' and the Nurse handed her the porridge and spoon.

A few minutes later, Jerry arrived, carrying a chair which he carefully placed on the other side of the bed. 'Hi – How's my Pheebs? Hope you had a real good sleep, baby.' He dropped his voice. 'Bad news today, Jane. Bloody Gooks, Vietnam – and they say there's been a massacre, a village called something like Me Lie – well, they all lie, and our Army's accused of attacking defenceless villagers, like any of them ever *are* "defenceless" – if it's even true about the attack, you never know these days – the media, *so-called* media, make up news all the time – ' He sat down heavily. 'Haven't got much time, they need me in the Office, I'm glad you're here now.' He looked at his watch. 'Ten minutes, that's all I got.'

Phoebe was trying to talk. 'Jane? Arnie? Eddie, Eddie –'

'Yes, my Brother, dear Phoebe. I know – Eddie – you and he–' How can I do this, how can I say what I'm trying to say? She carefully pushed a spoonful of porridge into Phoebe's mouth, and was relieved when it was safely swallowed.

A long pause. Then Phoebe suddenly said, loudly and clearly, 'But why didn't you love me the way you loved Arnie?'

Jerry stood up. 'Gotta go, sorry. It's her Father, she's been saying that a lot. About not loving her. Bye-bye, Pheebs, behave yourself! I'll be back later, and maybe we can eat dinner together, Jane, you and me, there's a half-good restaurant nearby, and I'll drop you off at the hotel after. Be seeing you!' He walked heavily to the door.

'It's about those Letters. They're on her mind. That's what I need to talk to you about, Jane.'

'Oh, I don't think –'

'Now, Jane, *no*! Do you think I don't know what's eating her up? I'm telling you it's those Letters. Before this happened, she would tell me how her Father, Sir Arthur Marston, I never met the guy of course, and I don't think her first husband, Homer was his name, did either, even when Sir Arthur was still alive – we got married, Pheebs and I, only last year, after my Winnie died and Pheebs divorced what's-his-name, her third husband – and she told me how Sir Arthur would say that *you* had all the Letters and stuff, his and his Mother's, as well as the Letters of the Red Baron, whoever he was, some sort of Communist? they're everywhere – and *you* would see about publishing them – but Pheebs was buggered up about that, she said she didn't see why her Father gave all those Letters to *you* in the first place, and not to *her*.'

'Well, a lot of them *were* to me. Arnold and I – well, we were all close friends, like Phoebe and Edwin. Not the Red Baron, of course, *those* letters were – So – And Olive Schreiner's and Hester, Sir Arthur's – I'm sorry Phoebe was upset about it, but her Father gave me the letters, for safe-keeping and, if possible, to get them published. But – '

'But you *didn't* get them published! Pheebs said that. And also it's – Well, I think it's partly because her Father – why did he favour *you*, why did he think she wasn't capable? – And yet she's smart, she's Vice-President of the Company, did she tell you that? She's *smart* and also very sensitive.'

Jane sat in silence. Then 'So what do you want me to do? I didn't *ask* to be given all those letters, in addition to the ones I already had, from my Brother, as well as from Phoebe's Brother. And in fact' Jane felt herself flushing and getting angry 'it's all been quite a burden over the years.'

'Well, why don't you send them to me, and I'll look after them for Pheebs? She'd like that, I know – and it might help her, fighting the cancer and all, give her another good reason to live.'

Again Jane was silent. Then she stirred, and sighed. 'It's – quite complicated. I'll – I'll have to think about it.'

'Not much time for that, baby. How's about tomorrow? You can think about it all tonight. You can dream about it! We'll talk tomorrow. It's decision time!'

Duty

*****

Back in her hotel room, Jane sat in front of the mirror that occupied most of the wall opposite a huge double-bed.

She was in deep thought. And trembling. 'All these years' she whispered to her reflected face 'and maybe it's time – really it's very simple, I suppose. Why is it a secret? Did *I* make it a secret? Edwin and Arnold – *they* didn't keep it secret, or did they? Was it Sir Arthur Marston, then? Or was it the moral and spiritual values of our society? So-called. I'd like to discuss all this with a Priest, but it's too late. And anyway, would it satisfy Phoebe to know the truth, after all these years? Or would it just throw her into greater turmoil? Would she blame me? But would it even be possible to discuss it all with her? Would she care? And what about *my* family – Julia, and especially Tom? Especially Tom.

But no more – I *must* sleep. Please. Exhaustion!

Chapter Twelve

'I can hardly bear to talk about it, or even *think* about it.'

The Police Officer waited politely, but after a few minutes said gently 'I can guess how you feel, Mrs Richardson, and I'm very sorry to press you on this. Would you like to take a break, have a coffee? Call your husband?'

'Oh, no, I couldn't do that, he's in his Lab, it's an extremely important experiment they're doing. Besides, this is all *my* responsibility – Mum would say that, if she could. And she did warn me – but who could possibly have expected, or even guessed? Literary Executor. When I agreed to do it, *try* to do it, I was mainly agreeing to take over what had become such a burden for her, more and more obviously after she turned seventy a few years ago. Tom didn't want to do it, he made that very clear, and nor did my children – even though, as I pointed out to them, some of the money – and there could be a lot, who knows? – would come to them. No, sorry to go on like this, Officer! It's just because I'm upset. Whether I like it or not, it's *my* responsibility. It's just that – Mum, how did it happen, how *could* it happen? And here, in this peaceful place where nothing ever happens.'

The Officer had been trained never to show any emotion, including impatience. He leaned forward. Then the door opened, and Julia's eighteen-year-old daughter Cassie appeared. 'Mum, what's happened?'

'Your Grandmother, she – '

'What, Mum? Is she all right?'

Julia tried to pull herself together. 'Darling. Gran has died.'

'How? How? When? I saw her just four days ago, she seemed fine.'

'Apparently – ' Julia looked pleadingly at the Officer, but he remained silent. 'Oh, darling, the Police say – They found her when a neighbour reported that the front door was open, which of course it never is, especially in winter – and then they followed tracks, hers and someone else's, they don't know whose – a man's, the Police think – and below that path above the river, they found – '

Jane's death brought publicity and speculation to the Village. How could such a thing happen here? *Nothing* ever happens here! Or not that sort of thing, anyway. But maybe it's connected somehow with the nearby murder of a man some people suspected of being a Russian spy?

The Police enquiries into Jane's death lasted some months, but produced no final answer; and gradually the incident fell back into silence. It was only when Cassie, during her career in Broadcasting, became the Host of a Current Affairs programme, that the silence cracked open and threw out possibly-relevant information. She contacted an ex-colleague, her predecessor.

'Hi. Trevor? How's it going? Oh, that's great! Yes, you warned me – I keep busy. And I'm sorting out all the stuff my Gran left – you warned me, and it sure did turn out to be quite the task! – Mum? Well, maybe she didn't have time, or inclination – my Mum keeps herself busy, she's a University Prof, here in the UK – yes, you know I'm a Brit, of course you do – and she did a lot of research, and still does – But I don't think she was interested in – well, I know she definitely did *not* want to be the Marston-Erlinger Literary Executor, it was only because my Uncle Tom totally refused to do it – And I remember how she used to complain about Researchers bugging her all the time, she hated that – but I also remember her telling Uncle Tom about the money that came, not much really, when books were published about Hester Marston – yes, right, she was that great early Feminist – and even her diaries and letters were published – but not any of the actual Marston-Erlinger First World War stuff because it had been embargoed for fifty years by my Grandmother – yes, that Jane Erlinger I told you about, I really don't remember much, I was a child when she was murdered, and they never found who did it – Anyway, Mum was deeply into Primary Education by then, trying to work out why kids like me had problems learning Maths and Science – Oh very clever, Trev! – But something that might interest you, remember that Unsolved Case, the last one in your second series? The guy who was found mysteriously dead in an English forest? – Yes, that one. Well, as I just said, my Gran was murdered, they think, some years back, and "in similar circumstances", as they say, near the same village – well, it's more like a town now – and it was a major mystery at that time. *Now* tell me you're not interested! Oh, you *are* interested! Surprise! Yes, of course it *would* fit into your new Unsolved Crime series, I'm sure it will. I'll rough out a preliminary script and fax it to you and you can exercise your, quote, "executive judgement". In other words, earn some of that big fat salary! Bye! Busy!'

Chapter Thirteen

Jane thought she heard a knock at the front door. Her hearing had noticeably deteriorated recently, she knew that – Maybe this was one of the grandchildren – but if it was Cassie, which it usually was, she would have telephoned in advance of her visit, and – She opened the door, a little breathless, and smiled apologetically. 'Sorry I was so long, I was in the kitchen.'

The man smiled. 'Oh, no problem!'

Flustered, she asked if he would care to come inside, out of the rain, and have a cup of tea with her. 'And I've just made some biscuits – cookies –' he seemed to be an American '– my grandchildren love them hot from the stove.'

Yes, he would like that. 'Thank you,' he said. 'I hope I'm not disturbing you?'

'No, no'. Was he another of those Researchers hoping to get permission to read the Correspondence? But he doesn't look or sound like one of those. 'Are you touring this area, Mr –?'

'Smith. Yes, it's sure a beautiful countryside, even in the rain. Not that it's raining heavily. Thank you for your hospitality, your cookies smell real good.' He deposited his umbrella and sat down. 'But I was hoping to – I am very interested in the Correspondence of English Combatants in the First World War – especially letters they wrote from the Front. That is why I came to Great Britain, at this difficult time – What do *you* think about it, the European Union? A time of decision! Will it be Yes or No? Do you think you can remain *Great* Britain if you try to keep separate from the rest of Europe? All those brave young Englishmen, like your Arnold and Edwin, who fought to save England from the Kaiser and his Krauts, over a hundred years ago – what would *they* think, how would *they* vote? – Now, these are *great* cookies, ma'am! Tea's not my thing, I always drink coffee, but this is *great* tea also!'

'Now, Dr – Smith. I think there's been a misunderstanding. I don't have those Letters you're wanting to see. They are all in a

University Library now, in Canada. I donated them. I can give you the University's address. But the Letters are embargoed for fifty years after my death. And as you see, I'm not dead yet.'

'But I guess you can give permission for me to *see* them – they were written to you and a Mrs Phoebe Hertz, who is deceased – but she quoted from some of them, in a book she wrote, and she said there were so many others, written by two of the young soldiers who were killed, Arnold and Edwin – and she said they were so important, they represented what it was really like in those trenches, and fighting in the mud on the Western Front – and so I – '

'Yes, yes. But, as I say, Dr Smith, they will not be available for consultation by *anyone* until some time after my death. The Librarian assured me of that.' – Jane was remembering the University Librarian who had come to talk to her about what he referred to as the Marston-Erlinger Papers, and how much his University was prepared to *pay* for the privilege of adding them to its burgeoning Pacifism Collection. It was quite a large sum! Which would make it possible for Tom's children to go to university? Yes, and *he* enjoyed my sandwiches and biscuits, said it was a privilege to have a Real English Tea, in an English home, said he'd never tasted Earl Grey before, and 'it's the perfect tea!' – I remember him saying that.

But mainly he quizzed me about Edwin and Arnold, and especially my relationship with Arnold – until I more-or-less accused him of being nosy, and then he laughed and apologized. And the Packers, is that what they were called? they came the next week, and were very efficient and polite – And, yes, Julia was right, what a relief! – a relief, after all those years, but also a *sadness* and almost emptiness, and also, just a bit of guilt? when they were finally gone.

He was looking hard at her; *glaring* at her.

She stood up hastily. 'Oh, Dr – Smith? – It looks as if the rain has stopped. And there's a beautiful view of the Valley from the path, it's not far from here – and then the path will take you down to the Village very directly – it's much quicker that way – and I can guide you as far as the look-out – '

The path was quite slippery after the rain. Jane led the way, in silence. She could hear the heavy breathing of her companion close behind. He's clearly very unhealthy, she thought. Not used to walking. Well, he's American.

'Look, here it is! This is the famous view!'

She half-turned towards him, as his heavy body struck hers.

When he had pulled himself upright, clinging to tree-branches, he was able to look down to where she lay, far below. Then he resumed walking, along the path to the village.

Chapter Fourteen

'Well, it's also an opportunity to see a bit of Canada – Toronto, it's near Toronto. Which is the capital of Ontario – I found it on the map. And the President of Masterson College was very insistent on the 'phone that I must come. She said that of course my knowledge of Great-Gran, and all those stories she told Gran that Mum told *me* when I was a girl, about Great-Uncle Edwin and his friend, Arnold I think his name was, they both died in the First World War – and those stories were *important*, the President said, and would definitely also be interesting to Graduate Students studying the History and Literature of the First World War. And of course, she said, they will pay for my trip – *everything*! I asked Brian if he'd like to do it, he knows so much more about all of that War stuff than I do; but he said he was too busy. So I agreed. As long as Mum would come with me, she really needs a holiday – and that was fine too! I'm quite looking forward to it – except for talking and answering questions. But Mum's good at that.'

'Great! I'm so glad for you, Janet. You deserve a holiday! Well, I do too, but nobody is offering to pay for me to have one, and with free accommodation too!'

'Also, as the President pointed out, I *am* the Literary Executor. I never wanted to be that, but Mum persuaded me to take over from her. I don't actually think that family-members should be able to prevent people reading and studying historic Letters and even prevent them being published – someone told me the other day that some Literary Editors just stop things being published by other people, so that *they* can publish them to make money and a reputation for themselves! Of course, because the main so-called Marston-Erlinger Letters have been Embargoed since 1970, there hasn't been a whole lot of Literary Executing to do ever since I took the job over from Mum – except to answer questions and occasionally give permission for the use of quotations, from other War-letters, and of course from the Hester Marston and Olive Schreiner Papers. Apparently there was great interest in the Marston-Erlinger Letters some years ago, by researchers into the First World War, after Arnold Marston's sister Phoebe published a book about when she was a Nurse in London during the War, and it included quotations from one or two of the Letters. But with the opening-up of *all* the Marston-Erlinger correspondence – well, the President says there will certainly be a great burst of new interest, and the University will encourage that by providing a lot of publicity. Their History Department is apparently agog!'

'So when are you leaving?'

'In a couple of months. After New Year. Didn't I tell you – I think I did – that 2020 is when the fifty-year Embargo of the Letters will end? My Great-Grandmother imposed it in 1969, when she sold the Papers, just before she died. Of course the University Library didn't like that at all, they said such a very lengthy Embargo was *extremely* unconventional and problematic, and they worked very hard to change her mind. But Mum says Great-Gran was adamant, and simply stated that of course all the rest of the Papers in the Collection would be open to Researchers – and if that University Library didn't want to accept her condition for selling them the Marston-Erlinger Papers, then they couldn't have any of the other Papers in the Archive, and she told them that other Libraries were interested and she'd donate *all* the Papers elsewhere. My Great-Gran was one feisty lady! But it has always been a big mystery, Arlene, in our family – why was she so insistent on that long Embargo. What is *in* those letters? Mum said she and *her* Mother, my Gran, tried very hard to find out, but just got nowhere – only smiles and silence – or "You'll find out one day, long after I've gone." And of course, because she was so old and frail, they didn't persist. But now, *soon*, we *will* find out.'

'And it could be a major disappointment.'

'Yes, it could. We'll see!'

* * * * *

The flight was, as they say, "uneventful". But Cassie, who had a long history of travel-sickness, was very glad when the taxi delivered them swiftly to their hotel in downtown Toronto. 'I must have a rest, Jan. I'm not as young as I was! You explore a bit, and tell me about your adventures in a couple of hours.'

They had chatted, while waiting at Heathrow for their flight, with an elderly English couple.

'Oh, we've done this quite often' the man had said. 'Our son and his wife and children, our grandchildren, they have lived there, in Burlington, near Toronto, for quite a few years. They love it there! And of course we take every opportunity to visit them. And especially now – ' He paused.

'Why "especially now"?' Janet asked.

'Well, you must have seen it on the news – speculation – a new Virus, maybe. Sounds like the one, what was it called? the one that – a few years ago – '

'SARS' his wife contributed. 'But don't ask me what its full name was. SARS was *terrible*! People died, hospitals struggled to cope – I remember it well, we were just glad to get back home to the U.K., but then we worried about our son and his wife and our grandchildren!'

'Well.' He grimaced. 'I heard it on the BBC News about this new Virus disease, it's in China somewhere, apparently, and they're worried now, the doctors and nurses and medical experts and of course the politicians, that it could even spread right round the world – much worse, maybe, than SARS.'

'Yes' Cassie replied. 'I did hear that on the CBC, but nobody seemed to know much about it. Hopefully they're wrong and they'll get it under control and it won't reach the West.'

Janet recalled that brief conversation as she wandered around downtown Toronto. Snow was falling gently. But everything looked to her like normal city-life – a lot of noisy traffic, including street-cars, she noted with interest – and pedestrians rushing carefully along crowded pavements – no, along *sidewalks*, not pavements, she corrected herself with a smile.

But – another Virus Pandemic? – Could something like that actually happen? Surely not. In 2020! Our medical facilities must be much better now at tracking, controlling and defeating a disease like SARS. It's just one of those rumours. Something Trump tweeted which he'll contradict tomorrow.

Oh but I'm flagging! I think I must be following Mum into jet-lag – better get back to the hotel, have an early supper and go to bed for a really good sleep!

The President was, according to Cassie's comment later, severe-looking but 'all smiles'. She came immediately to greet them after her Secretary rang through to her the news that her two important English visitors had arrived.

'Oh, great to see you, did you have a good flight?' as she shook hands. 'Now, let me tell you that we have arranged a little preliminary event tomorrow morning, ahead of the two Presentations in the evening, and after lunching with me at the Faculty Club you'll be free to spend time in our Special Collections, where Library Staff will be pleased to answer any questions you may have. But first – I hope you had a comfortable ride here from Toronto, in our Visitors' Transport? Oh but please do sit down and make yourselves comfortable, the coffee will be served momentarily. And after lunch I'll drive you to the hotel, it's not far away, just as soon as you like. Or my Assistant can show you round the Library and campus first.'

'Thank you, we're so glad to be here. I'm Janet, we've had some correspondence. And this is my Mother, Dr Catherine Richardson, she preceded me as Literary Executor of my Great-Grandmother Jane's Papers.'

'I'm delighted to meet you both. And of course you will both know what an auspicious occasion this is for us, and the Researchers and many others who have been waiting impatiently for the day on which all of the Marston-Erlinger Archive will be opened to all Readers, after being embargoed for fifty years!' The President paused, to take a breath. 'There's very great anticipation and, yes, excitement, at Masterson – in several Departments. National and local media have also of course been informed, and expressed interest and anticipation, and will be in attendance at your Presentation tomorrow – for which, I might say, I will be Chairperson – so I'm going to say, right now, we are hoping that *both* of you, as Present and Past Literary Executors, will be gracious enough to speak and answer questions, not only about the Papers and the circumstances of their writing, but also about the relationships among the writers and original readers of the Letters, and, of course, the Great War connection.' The President paused again, looking at them expectantly.

As Janet readied herself to answer, Cassie said firmly 'Yes, of course, we'll do our best. But remember, we aren't Historians, just relatives, descendants, of the Writers. Like you and your Students, we can only know Edwin Erlinger and Arnold Marston through the words they wrote, all that time ago. In a different world, and in desperate circumstances. The First World War. Bombs, poison gas, and mud, mud, mud!'

'Yes. The horrors of war. Our generation has been spared, so far. And we must hope – But there is another topic we should discuss briefly, since, again, it involves the Erlinger-Marston Archive. And again is a reason to express deep gratitude to you both and the Erlinger and Marston families, and, above all, to Jane Erlinger. You know where I'm going?'

Cassie smiled. 'I think so. You're moving from War to Feminism. Am I right?'

'Yes. Yes. Perhaps the gratitude of this University has never been fully expressed for your family's generosity, and I'd like to at least begin remedying that. Did you realise, any of you, the huge importance of the Hester Marston and Olive Schreiner Archives? Well, this University didn't either, at first. So many years after the Suffragettes! But without those Archives I seriously doubt that this University would now have a Department of Feminism and an often-acknowledged world-class reputation in the teaching and study of Feminist thought and writing. I say this, too, as a worker in that field – '

'President Macey – '

'Oh, call me Jess. Please. Everybody does!'

'Jess.' Cassie and Janet glanced smilingly at each other. 'Jess. We know of your high reputation, as a Scholar, and a founding member of World Women, and we have both of us read and enjoyed and been impressed by your recent book *Women of the World*. So – '

'Oh, let me finish this – I have been wanting to say this for so long! It's my duty. Catherine and Janet, if I may use your first names – it is a pleasure and honour, a great pleasure and a great honour, to welcome you here, as descendants and representatives of Jane Erlinger, who made it possible. Made what possible? The very existence of our Department of Feminism. Literally! I don't think I exaggerate. When I and other scholars of Feminism, who had mainly and for some years studied and researched Feminism in the United States and Europe – when we explored the Schreiner and Marston Archives, and realized what riches they contained, we pressed, we *campaigned*, for the establishment of what is now our internationally-respected Feminism Department, in this University – and a large part of our success came about because of those Archives. Because they provided, indisputedly, a scholarly basis and opportunity for research in Feminism. I wonder if Jane Erlinger could have believed that? In her day, the two World Wars and their merely political effects loomed much larger around the world! Much larger than the dire situation of women. But now, partly – or even perhaps *largely* – as a result of Feminist influence and discourse, Peace is dominant, and has helped to create the increasing impetus to resolve other pressing international issues, such as Climate Change.'

The President stopped talking, and, realizing that she was sitting uncomfortably at the edge of her chair, sat back and looked searchingly at Cassie and Janet. Who were smilingly silent.

Then, after taking a deep breath, the President said 'More coffee?' Then 'Well, that's Jane Erlinger's contribution to Feminism. Not just Pacifism – *Feminism!* Sorry if I have seemed over-enthusiastic. I guess I'm still a novice President! But we'll come back to that topic – I've started the ball rolling for a Conference next year on Forms of Early Feminism, featuring the Schreiner and Marston Archives. So – Prepare yourselves for a summons!'

Janet said 'Oh, that will be –'

'But now, back to War! Duty calls.' The President was on her feet. 'And I see the hour approaches for Lunch – which of course takes precedence over both War *and* Feminism, and demands Peace and Sustenance. Follow me, friends! To what used to be called the Powder Room.'

Chapter Fifteen

The telephone rang. 'Hullo. Is this Jane –?' An unfamiliar female voice.

'Oh. Yes it is. Do you want my daughter, I'm afraid she's – '

'No. I'm Nurse Howells. I'm telephoning on behalf of Sir Arthur Marston. He wonders if you are free to visit him. If so –'

'Oh, yes, of course. Is it urgent? I could walk over – '

'No, not urgent. But he would like you to visit him this afternoon, if that's convenient. I could drive over in an hour or so and bring you to him.'

'Oh. Yes, fine. Thank you. I'll be ready.'

Jane could tell that this was not a routine invitation. She had visited Sir Arthur a few days earlier, and had noted his pallor and trembling hands. When she was leaving, he had suddenly said 'Dear Jane – ' and when she turned to smile goodbye he had said again, more loudly, 'Dear Jane – Goodbye, thank you for coming.'

As they drove towards Marston House, Nurse Howells said 'I couldn't say this over the 'phone because I thought he might hear. Sir Arthur will be going into hospital tomorrow for an operation. You may not know, because he has made it clear that nobody was to be told, that he has been suffering from cancer for several months. But I'm sure you do know that his wife died last year, and his son during the War. He has been struggling with grief and painful memories, and has requested isolation. Which has been a concern to his doctor and myself. So we are relieved that he wishes to have your presence – an old friend, he said. I would only request that you stay with him for no more than, say, an hour at most. And here we are.'

'Yes, I understand' Jane said. We are all dying, she thought; Arnold, Edwin – my beloved Edwin; and now what we have feared for so long, what we have been working so hard to prevent, and it seems to come closer and closer – war, war again, more death, more suffering –

* * * * *

Sir Arthur was sitting up in bed, supported by several pillows. 'Jane, my dear Jane. Thank you for coming. Again.' His voice was husky, weak. 'Sorry I can't entertain you better.'

She sat in the chair beside him. Then stood up to kiss him gently on his forehead. Thinking I never did anything like this before, but now – and she took one of his cold hands in hers – 'Sir Arthur, I'm so glad to see you' – if I'm not careful I'll start weeping, which would embarrass both of us. He looks so weak – pale and weak.

He cleared his throat. 'Actually, my dear, this is a business meeting of sorts. I need to say some things to you. Things I should have said before. So it's – off the record, as it were.' His voice had strengthened slightly. There was a pause.

'But, Sir Arthur, I need to say some things to *you*. That I should have said long ago. First – thank you, I am so grateful – *thank you* for all your kindness to me and my family over so many years. And for all that you have done for me personally – and I'm not just thinking of your generosity – the house, and your friendship, your kindness – and when my father – and to my children, especially Tom – but also your concern – the letters – '

'Oh, and there are more, you'll curse me eventually – Do you know why? I don't think I ever said, Jane. Your love for Arnold and his for you. Yes. And the kindness you always showed to my dear wife, our Mutti, and to my daughter Phoebe.' He paused and cleared his throat. 'About *her*, about Phoebe, I feel guilty, Jane. I wonder if I caused all her hostility and rejection. Yes, I did – I know I did. You see – She always reminded me of my Mother – in appearance and behavior – in so many ways. Did you know –? Yes, if you have read her diaries, and her letters to me and my Father – then you will know that my Mother rejected us both and threw in her lot with the Suffragettes, Mrs Pankhurst and her lot. So she abandoned my Father, and me. I see now that they had some right on their side, the Suffragettes

– and of course I don't know all that went on in my parents' marriage, but – did it *have* to be hurtful, so *absolute*, the way we were treated – total rejection – I was just a boy, and yet my Mother seemed to think I could cope with her rejection of me and my Father – well, he was humiliated, of course, and he never recovered. He suffered. Dreadfully. I never told you that I very nearly burnt all her letters and diaries – if you hadn't been looking after Arnold and Edwin's letters I would have burnt my Mother's. But – oh, I didn't mean to offend you, Jane – I know you – '

'I'm not offended, Sir Arthur. But please don't cause yourself strain.' Jane took his other hand in both her hands: it was cold, so she rubbed it gently.

After a few moments, 'And Edward' he continued quietly. 'Edward. After Arnold was taken from me, Edward – he was my son as well as your brother. You must have seen that.'

'Yes' she said. 'I did. And you did so much for him, you gave him encouragement, and support. He was so grateful, I know, and so was I. And then you gave *me* so much support, after Mum died – and Tom, you made me promise never to tell him about the support you have given *him* – the School, and Balliol, and – you made me promise never to tell him and I never did – Oh, Sir Arthur – so much, you did so much for us all. How can I –?'

Then she noticed that his eyes had closed and his head was hanging forward. She carefully placed his hands under the blanket. Should I just leave quietly? No – Phoebe – But maybe I should call the Nurse first, he looks so uncomfortable now.

Nurse Howells lowered Sir Arthur gently in the bed until he was lying comfortably against his pillow. Then she turned to Jane. 'I'm afraid he's fast asleep, we won't disturb him. Let me ask the maid to come and sit beside him while I drive you home.'

PART FIVE
Chapter Sixteen

Saturday 1st February 2020

And, approaching from the East, a new Plague. The world collapsing? Soon its populations will tremble, endure isolation, fear death. Society is ending, it's all ending.

So is there any point in guessing, or even finding out, *knowing*, what happened, over a century ago, in one corner of the planet, before and during one war? Especially regarding minor personal relationships and other occurrences, some of which may once have seemed major and potentially influential; and destructive, even consequential? No – you say No? Are we all now living in Trumpland – or mired in the worst Disney movie, the one entitled 'How Goes It in that Exceptional Nation, that Paradigm, that Greatest of all Nations that have ever existed, or *could* ever exist: the United States of America?' And the rest of planet Earth, too: how goes it? Oh, and has all Truth become *truly, finally* Fake?

Well, then I'm free to end this story for you, however it wants to be ended. You desire more than one ending? Oh, feel free – two, eleven, forty-nine, ninety-seven, however many you desire, or think you desire. It's your choice! This is the Land of Fake-History. And I am your Fake-Narrator.

So let's go! I'll keep the basic plot-line (you've been following it, or trying to, through all the words composing Parts One to Four, Chapters One to Fifteen, of this Fake-Narrative).

And please forgive my pullulating fear and bitterness. It *is* justified. Will *be* justified. Elsewhere.

How the Marston-Erlinger Papers evolved you will have already noted (*if* you were attentive while reading the earlier Parts of this narrative!).

I will summarise. The Papers consist, primarily, of letters written by two schoolboy friends (Arnold Marston and Edwin Erlinger) and by their sisters (Jane Erlinger and Phoebe Marston). The Correspondence begins just after the First World War commenced in 1914 and continues until the two friends were killed, separately, in front-line combat. Subsequently, other Papers were attached (notably relating to the so-called Red Baron, to Olive Schreiner, and to Sir Arthur Marston and his Mother Hester), and so are included in a Collection formed under the purview of the late Jane Erlinger, named above. She sold the Papers to Masterson University Library in 1969, before her death; with the addition of her personal diaries and other material, but also with the stipulation that the entire Marston-Erlinger Correspondence be embargoed for 50 years. That embargo ended a few weeks ago, on January 1st, 2020.

So now!

'Welcome to you all! I am Gordon Allen, the University Librarian.

'As you will all know, the President of Masterson College, which received the Marston-Erlinger Archive in 1970, is about to deliver a Speech celebrating the Opening of the Complete Papers, at the Conclusion of the fifty-year Embargo imposed by the Donor, Ms Jane Erlinger. The Donor's grand-daughter Dr Catherine Richardson, and great-grand-daughter Ms Janet Fairley, will then Comment and Answer Questions posed by Members of the Audience. After lunch, two Papers will be presented, one by a member of the Masterson History Department, Dr Lily Buttridge, and the other by eminent Australian critic William Shirley. The Occasion will conclude with a Celebratory Dinner tonight, in the University Buttery. But now – President Macey, who of course needs no introduction.'

'Thank you, Dr Allen. And may I welcome our Distinguished Guests: Dr Catherine Richardson and Ms Janice Fairley, descendants and Literary Executors of Jane Erlinger who come to us from the UK; Vice-President Melanie Ferencz; Dean of Literary Arts Arthur Hartley; Associate Dean Herbert Grasse, and Chair of History Maryanne Stager; Visiting Colleagues; Members of the National and International Media; and Friends. Welcome, on this auspicious occasion. Welcome, indeed!

'Fifty years ago, our Library acquired what has become known as the Marston-Erlinger Archive, from Ms Jane Erlinger, twin-sister of Edwin Erlinger. For over half-a-century she had diligently preserved the Papers, before deciding that they should be placed in an eminent University Library in North America, to be made available for international research.

'She had also insisted, however, on Embargoing any Correspondence by or to Arnold Marston and Edwin Erlinger, and by Sir Arthur Marston and herself. And further – I was made aware of this only a few hours ago, when the boxes containing the Letters were opened – she had demanded that their availability, after the fifty-year Embargo ended, should be preceded by the public reading of a Personal Document that she had added as a Preface to the Correspondence. This further requirement is, to my knowledge, not only unusual but probably unprecedented. However, I believe we should now acknowledge and fulfil her request, not only in gratitude for her prescient generosity but also to ensure that the Embargo has been fulfilled and cannot be legally challenged in the future. Are there any objections to my recommendation? No – No? Then I request Dr Grasse, the University's Public Orator, to read Ms

Erlinger's Personal Document, entitled, I believe, "The Complete Truth At Last".

Dr Grasse (holding the text close to his eyes, and with some lengthy pauses):

The Complete Truth at Last. 5th January, 1970.
'My second Great-Grand-daughter, who will be christened Janet, after her Father's favourite Aunt, has just been born, and I have been told that she is without blemish! Deo gracias. Tom's two sons, or one of them, may yet produce children, but I can't wait for that. He is gone, and Phoebe is gone, and I know that now it is almost time for me to go too. I have had a very long, and latterly a pleasant, tranquil life – which is not the usual experience of us members of the War Generation – survivors of the Great War of 1914–1918, I mean, of course, not the Second Great War of 1939–1945 – although that was also horrendous, even if the combatants didn't die in extreme pain in muddy trenches or from poison gas.

'But pull yourself together now, Jane. And I hope that you who are reading this can decipher my shameful scrawl – also my pen keeps slipping out of my trembling hand, alas. But – Gumption, Jane!

'What I have to say may shock you. I'm sorry. But then, remember that I have carried it around in my brain and heart for how many years? More than fifty – many more years than those two boys had in their lives. Edwin, my twin Brother, and his dear friend Arnold, who I also loved. They were almost the same age. School-friends – and that is a relationship that we can hardly imagine now, I think – so close, so intense. That's what I and Arnold's sister, Phoebe, who was two years younger than me, observed, and tried to understand. She was at a sort of Public Boarding School too, for girls, there were a few of those, if your parents could afford it. Edwin and I were very close when we were small, and Edwin and Arnold too, and then Edwin was sent to the same Public School as Arnold – probably Sir Arthur Marston, Arnold's Father, helped our Father with the fees, I think he really liked and approved of Edwin, who had been close friends with Arnold since they were small boys and played together in the Park. Of course I was sent to a nearby day-school for girls, and when I was cross I thought how that was so very unfair, and prejudiced, and that it must be so I could be expected to help in the housework, cooking and washing-up, and delivering messages and so on. Things have changed such a lot, haven't they? But when we got together at first, the four of us, Edwin and Arnold and Phoebe and me, in the early summer of 1914 – I remember it was at a House cricket-match, Arnold and Edwin were both very good cricketers, as well as being very clever – and Edwin was also very musical – he composed some piano-music and they both wrote poetry. Well, we really "hit it off", the four of us, and became close friends. Also Daddy worked for Sir Arthur, Arnold's father, and the two of them were sort-of-friends too at that time. But none of all this lasted. The War came, and first Arnold and then Edwin – oh, it's still so painful, so painful, to remember – they were both killed, fighting the Germans on the Western Front – which was devastating for Phoebe and me. We suffered. And both families suffered. Of course, there was a lot of suffering everywhere, and not just of soldiers, but wives and parents and siblings and friends –

'Sometimes – What happened with Mum and Dad, it was so sad also – and then Arnold was killed, and then even Edwin, right near the end of the War when I thought he would survive, he must survive. Well, he didn't. And I had to go on, alone. Except for Tom, but he was a baby then, he couldn't – of course he couldn't understand. And not only Eddie and Arnie were gone, which was dreadful, unbearable, and still is, but also Mum and Dad. She died soon after the War started. It was a terrible shock – I knew that she was ill, of course, and she was in hospital – but then – she died in child-birth, and I didn't even know she was pregnant, nobody told me, nobody did tell you those things then, we didn't even have any idea of sex, what sex really is, we girls – the boys learnt it all at school, and sort of did it with each other. How could I have been so ignorant? But I truly was.

'So Mum died in child-birth. And then Dad was a total mess, I think he blamed himself for Mum's death – and he held me and held me, night after night, even during the day sometimes – so tight, as if he was drowning and that I would be able to save him. But I couldn't. So often I still tell myself that surely, surely I could have done more, for both my parents. But – there was Tom, he was a baby. And so I became his Mother. Sir Arthur was so kind to me, he got me a nurse, and then a maid, to help me until I could look after him on my own. And he paid them, and then a bit later, after Daddy was gone, and Arnold had been killed, he bought this house, which Daddy had rented – and he put it in my name – so I didn't have to pay any rent, and he even made a Settlement, is that the right word? – 'So you'll never be in want', he said. Why did he do all that? Of course he never said, even when I asked him once or twice, but I sort-of knew – I knew it was because of Arnold being killed, he was gassed early in the War – and that we loved each other, Arnold and I – and of course because of Tom – and also it was because of Daddy – because he just left, he just went away, about a year after Mum's death, or was it later, and I never knew what happened to him, and I also feel guilty about that. Did he die all on his own? I don't even know where his grave is, but I always go to Mum's grave, and put flowers on it. I think Sir Arthur must have known that Dad hurt me, he must have seen my bruises even though I tried to hide them from him, from everybody – But why did Daddy do it, did he blame me somehow for Mum's death? as well as blaming himself – I wondered and wondered about that – but really there wasn't very much time to wonder about anything, I had to learn to be a Mother, and I did – and every time Tom called me 'Mummy' I had to try not to cry. He grew up to be a good man, and a good son, and a good older-brother for Julia, especially after her Father left me for another woman – but Julia was grown-up by then. And Sir Arthur even *paid for Tom to go to the same School that Edwin and Arnold went to. And then, in the Second War, Tom was a Spitfire Pilot in the Battle of Britain, one of those who saved us from Hitler and the Nazis. The bravest of the brave. I was so proud of him. But he died fifteen years or so after the War, heart-attack.*

'So now I've told most of what happened. But about the Boys' letters. I kept them all, the ones I had, and then also the ones Sir Arthur gave me – he knew that I would keep them just as carefully as the ones Arnold had written to me – and I think also he didn't want them around, he wanted to forget about the War maybe, as much as possible, after Arnold was killed – his only son. And I think he knew how much we loved each other, Arnold and me. But of course he couldn't forget completely, and every year he was in the Remembrance Parade, and he would take me with him most years, if I could go – I wondered if he remembered that Speech Day in 1914 and how he made a speech saying the Boys must fight if England and the British Empire was attacked – maybe he even regretted that Speech later, after Arnold died, and Edwin, and so many other Schoolboys – but of course, if he did, he would never say that.

'But I was going to say about the Letters – and then I'm finished, which will be a relief, to you and to me, my hand is getting very sore, and probably your eyes! – I was going to say that, quite often I nearly persuaded myself to burn the Letters, get rid of them completely. The things about Dad and me especially – and Mum's death, and about Tom. But I don't think I have said how very very painful and sad those things were – and in some of the letters between Arnold and Edwin, they show it. But I feel so guilty about that, too. I should have kept quiet. But once, after Daddy attacked me – And he would be drunk too, often, I could smell it on his breath – Well, Edwin was out of the military hospital, he had to have a small operation, I can't remember why, maybe appendix, and when he was better, and back in the Army, he thought he might be able to come home for just a few days, to see us, before going overseas to France with his Regiment – and

I don't think he'd even seen Tom at all, and he didn't know about Dad, of course, so I thought I must warn him – because Dad was becoming more and more violent – but I must have said too much – and when he couldn't come – or maybe he did, just for a few hours, I can't remember – and before that he wrote to Arnold, and in that letter – I couldn't bear to read it again now – Well, he asked Arnold to tell his Father, and ask him to stop Dad doing what he was doing to me, and I think that's why he went away, Daddy, I mean – he just – he just vanished.

'*So here is the whole Correspondence that has survived – letters mainly between Edwin and me, and Arnold and me, also some letters to each other, or by and to other members of our two families. Whenever anyone asked me, over all those years, why I was keeping them, I would say 'Because it's my* duty.' *And also a lot of letters by other young soldiers – most of them had been school-friends of Edwin and Arnold – those letters were given to me by Sir Arthur Marston.*

'*And so now my duty is done. Actually, I hate that word. Duty! Is it ever a duty to maim or kill our fellow-humans? Or fellow-animals? How can it be? So – Before you decide that I'm crazy – And in conclusion – at last, you say, and I say it too! – I say that I hope that these letters will be of historical value to researchers, and maybe help to show again, for anyone who doubts, how deadly and destructive and painful War is. War! It took from me both the Boys I loved. I loved Arnold, and I loved Edwin – so very much. Maybe what has been written in the Letters will inspire us to cry out loudly, and ever more loudly, as loudly as possible, NO MORE WAR! NO MORE WAR! NO MORE WAR!*

'Jane Erlinger'

In the silence following Dr Grasse's reading, the President stood, and moved to the microphone.

'Thank you. That was a marathon – Dr Grasse, you must be breathless. To read aloud, without preparation, an extensive, unfamiliar, handwritten text is a great challenge, and I'm sure you acquitted yourself in the task very much better than anyone else in this room could have done. Thank you again.

'Are there any comments or questions before we break for lunch, and then reassemble for the presentation of the two Papers? As there is only time for a few questions, I have decided to delay my own presentation, which now be a prelude to the two major Papers that we are so much looking forward to this afternoon.'

Cassie, who had been sitting in tense silence, stood up.

'I think you can see how moved we both are, Janet and I, hearing those emotional words written so long ago by a loved and admired relative, who died when I was just over thirty and my daughter Janet was just a small child. Jane Erlinger was a remarkable woman in so many ways. She helped so many people. That was her *duty*, she would always say. She was certainly dutiful! And much more – she did so much, quietly and sometimes anonymously, for various causes and for so many people. She was one of those indispensable people! But also she was rather secretive about her early life, as I think my daughter would agree.' And she smiled down at Janet.

'We are so anxious to read the Letters that have now come out of Embargo, and I know other members of our family will feel the same way. But most of all, we are glad to know that Jane Erlinger's hard work and dedication, in preserving Letters not only of great personal but also of great historical value, have now been honoured, just as she had hoped. And *we* hope that they will be read by many, especially young students, and *used* by historians to remind us all about the consequences of War.

'It is a pleasure to be here, Madame President. Janet and I will be happy to answer any questions as we are able. Thank you, thank you, again.'

She sat down. And after a moment Janet added quietly 'My Mother has said it all. Thank you.'

CPSIA information can be obtained
at www.ICGtesting.com
Printed in the USA
BVHW032101010521
606176BV00001B/49